The Half-Sighted

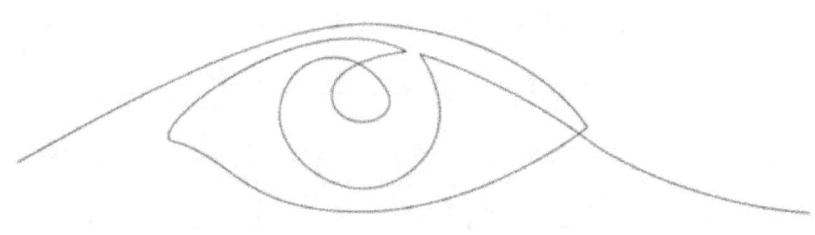

M. Stamm

THE HALF-SIGHTED

ISBN: PB: 978-1-0690169-4-2, EB: 978-1-0690169-5-9, H: 978-1-0690169-6-6

Imprint: Independently published

THE MIRROR UNIVERSE
YA Fantasy

The Half-Sighted
The Vampires
The Wanderers
The Ancients

Also by Morena Stamm...

NAMED AGAIN SERIES
Dark Fantasy

Ashta the Lion Tamer
Svetlana the Last Princess
Darkling the Broken Slave

Coming soon...
Trice the Wolf Hunter

To my younger self.
Every nightmare ends where a dream
begins.
So, never stop dreaming.

PROLOGUE

"Order. Order. I said ORDER."

The dark lit room finally quieted enough to allow the speaker to continue.

"Now as I said before, there are people—many of which are in this room right now—that agree that something must be done. We cannot allow this kind of action to continue within our very walls." His ancient voice trembled with both fear and hunger. He knew what the child was capable of.

If he was a younger man...

But he wasn't.

He stared each of the other councilmen in the eyes. Many nodded in assent. A few near the back stayed still. Malika and Dominstadi. They had known the child's mother and were leery to do anything more.

"It must be done. In the name of the first world, the second and the great beyond." His voice shook through the walls as everyone looked up at him. Finally.

"Alkira *Vincit Omnia*."

The speaker glanced over at the middle-aged man. He liked the councilman's dedication. Even his fervor for the protection of Alkira. But at times, he worried about the crazed look in the younger man's eyes.

"Alkira *Vincit Omnia!*"

Another young councilman yelled, a close friend of the first. The speaker worried his chin as the two men riled up the rest of the group. To soon everyone but the speaker and the two councilmen in the back were yelling Alkira in unison.

Aye. Alkira.

His gaze took in the scene. He had lived long enough to know some of her secrets. Enough to know that what the men were playing with right now could very well end all of the universes.

"Enough!"

His voice shook through the men as the two councilmen who started the rally cry stood stock-still. The speaker looked both of the men in the eye before giving them a slight nod. Satisfied the two men took a seat, silent once more.

"Now with that matter decided for, let's move onto the next order of..."

Not long after the speaker left the small room, the councilman left as well.

"Dimtri!" A loud whisper bounced across the stonewalls. The councilman whipped around and held the other councilman by the throat.

"How many times have I told you, don't use my name!" he whispered back. He watched the fear swimming in the other man's eyes with satisfaction. One day, he would have the entire council watching him with the same fear. The thought excited him.

But until then, the need for secrecy was imperative.

He released the other man, watching as his body slid to the ground. With a grunt the councilman stepped over his body and continued on his way. He needed to hurry. Bruchkova would find him later. Whatever he wanted to speak of was nowhere near as important as what *he* needed to do.

A few twists and turns through the stone maze of the caves finally led him to an old cavern. Stalagmites rose as great teeth gnashing at the caves ceiling. The boy better be here.

The quiet drips from the stalactites hit his already tight nerves, the tension screeching off of his body.

There. A quiet shuffle. He turned in time to watch the boy's cocky saunter. His hair was spiked back and gleamed like his moms. And yet he was half-sighted.

"You wanted to speak with me, sir?"

Even his voice was cocky, and too loud for the echoing cavern. He winced before turning to the side, forcing the boy to come closer to hear him.

The young man walked closer, his shoulders hunched with tension. Good.

"It's done."

For a moment the boy just watched him. Then his eyes widened, and his face paled before finally settling into stone.

"Is that all?" he asked, his voice scratchy with emotions.

The councilman stepped closer to the boy until that slight widening of his eyes finally gave way to fear. That's all he wanted from the boy. Nothing more.

"You follow him, and you make sure it's done."

With that he shouldered past the boy. He hadn't made it two steps before the boy called back to him. "And if he survives?"

The councilman stopped but refused to turn around, keeping the power of the conversation with himself. "Then don't bother coming back until it *is* done."

And with that he walked away for good.

The boy watched him leave with a heavy heart. It wasn't what he wanted. But it was the first time the councilman trusted him with something important. He couldn't screw this up. Because if he did... No. He didn't want to think about that.

He wouldn't screw it up. And he wouldn't come back until it was done. Even if it broke his heart. With a grim face, he followed the councilman's steps back to the main caves before disappearing into the night.

CHAPTER 1

¢

Trees whip and scratch at my face as if trying to claw away my speed. But I don't let them. I can feel the Shade close behind me as I push past the underbrush.

At least the Shade is here rather than back on Alkira. It would be a lot harder to hide from the courts attention if a Shade was found at home. I shudder at the thought, as my mom hasn't made an effort to leave the house for over a decade.

I push my legs harder, feeling the burn of my hamstrings singe away the imaginings of blood-spattered eggshell walls.

The darkness here is eerie. Almost heavy. Not even a moon in the sky. Just leaves above, below, and all around. My heart beats in time with my pounding feet.

Finally, a light. The heaviness in the air here makes it hard to breathe. A humidity I am not used to. At least there *is* air to breathe in this world.

Be thankful for the little things.

Clearing the brush, for a moment I'm taken aback by the sight in front of me. A long smooth single stone road with poles lining the sides that have a light somehow attached to them.

The inner tinker in me wants to stop and take a closer look—it looks like something from our history books—but the survivalist pushes past the novelty as the distinct crackle of breaking tree limbs comes closer.

Fuck it.

I decide to go left, taking the middle of the smooth road. For some reason there are long lines painted there.

I don't have long to wonder. Right now, I need to put as much distance between me and the Shade as possible.

Slap.

Slap.

Slap.

My shoes echo through the still night, in a strange harmony with my strangled breaths. I should have taken a running elective this year rather than the natural design class.

Too late now.

A buzzing can be heard in the distance ahead. But it quickly morphs into a loud hum before becoming a roar.

I only have time to cover my face as a bright light swings around the corner ahead on the road.

CRASH.

Darkness.

"Oh my god, are you alright?"

Groaning I take stock of vitals. Breathing. *Check.* Heartbeat. *Check.* Can feel my legs and arms? Overly so. My left leg in particular is screaming at me. It'll be bruised for sure.

A cool touch wisps across my forehead. I open my eyes and all I can see is dark holes rimmed in desert gold and burning blue skies.

And then it blinks.

Jerking back, I forget my pain for moment.

"Hey you're bleeding! Let me help you. The hospital is not far."

Coughing, I push myself onto my knees before awkwardly standing.

"No need. I'm alright."

"Alright? You're insane!"

I look up at her in shock as her concern shifts into anger.

"What the *fuck* were you thinking running down the *middle* of the road wearing nothing but *black*? At night!?"

"Uh..."

"You weren't thinking! That's what!"

A rustle from the bushes. Crap. The bright lights from the crash seem to be attached to some sort of grounded moving machine.

"I need a ride."

"Like hell I'm going to drive you anywhere but straight back to the hospital." She crosses her arms, her eyes spitting fire at me.

Glancing back at the darkness, I turn toward her. "You don't understand, something is chasing me and if you don't help me, we are both going to die."

She raises an eyebrow in disbelief. "Who do you take me for? This is Ponoka, not some horror movie set."

"Look, you won't understand but—" Before I can get another word out her eyes widen as she looks over my shoulder. She lets out an ear-splitting scream, stopping the Shade in its tracks for a moment.

Grabbing her shoulders I shake her. "We need to leave. Now."

She just nods wordlessly, pointing me to the other side of the machine. Its shape tickles my memory. I've seen it before. I slide over to the front, opening the door and slamming it behind me as I sink into the plush stained seats.

A moment after the girl slams her own door, cranks the stick between us back and stomps her foot. That's when I realize; I'm in a car. An ancient machine from the fifth cycle of dArs. *I was right!* *I can't believe I'm sitting in one instead of studying it in class!*

Suddenly we are in motion as I watch the Shade shrink in the distance. Then in horror, I watch as it's strange arms curl under it with great-serrated claws, each the size of a scythe, and it leaps forward toward us.

"Hurry up!" I yell, as the Shade claws its way closer.

"I'm hurrying, I'm hurrying!"

A screech like the sound of a hundred fabrics being torn at once fills the night air.

The girl's knuckles go white on the steering wheel. She looks up at me, her face set as stone.

"Hold on."

I brace myself on the ceiling and the door. Just as the Shade gets within leaping distance, the girl stomps on the gas and pulls up the emergency brake. For a moment my face is plastered against the window, and then we are going forward.

She shifts and the engine growls as trees hurtle past us faster.

"Where to?" she asks. Houses pass on the left of us.

"As far away as possible."

She looks over at me as the car slows to a stop.

Glancing up in the mirror, she turns left and the car lurches forward.

"The two isn't far from here."

I just nod, my attention caught by all the lights in front of me on the inside. I have only ever seen holopics of a car, but the model was very different to the one I sit in now.

"You're not from around here, are you?"

I push in a button and noise blasts out from all around us. Covering my ears I yell, "how do you stop it?"

She reaches forward and turns the volume back down. Cool. She swats my hand away before I can touch any other buttons. I decide to look out the windows instead. We cross over a bridge, an ancient locomotion with rusted grain cars below us.

It always fascinated me the technologies that are present from one world to the next. Trains I am familiar with. It is how the four courts are connected. One big loop connecting all four corners of Alkira.

"What do you call this planet?"

The light poles pass us by as we glide over and down the hill. The girl squints at me before returning her gaze to the road.

"Earth."

Nodding, I go back to studying the inside of the car.

"And this car we are currently sitting in?"

"A ford."

"And do all aford's look like this?"

She snorts before replying, "Its ford, no a. And no, there are cars, vans, trucks, SUV's. Then there's the sports models, they look entirely different."

"How does it work—"

She waves me off. "Hold on. Before we go talking about the mechanics of a car, we need to talk."

"Are we not talking already?"

"Ha ha, smart ass." I can't help but grin at her sarcasm. Feisty. Not that I expect much else from someone whose hair is bright red. Like the colour of a big shiny apple, the kind I always bought for Kian's birthday.

"Okay, let's start with the basics. What's your name?"

"Does it matter?"

"I just ran you over and saved your ass from some...thing... and for all I know you could be some creepy serial killer or alien waiting to abduct me."

She has quite the imagination on her. The alien reference hits a little close to the heart. I never much liked the word. I *am* human, just from another universe.

"My name is Jared. I've never killed another human being much less kidnapped one."

"So, what you're saying is you *are* an alien."

"No."

We come to a stop ahead of a set of lights. Except these ones are red.

"Look, Jared, if I'm going to be driving you somewhere, I need to know I can trust you first."

My fingers tap without my consent on the armrest. The sidelights are green. As I watch, they shift to orange. The car moves as the lights ahead of us turn green.

Green, go. Red, stop.

I can't help but chuckle.

"What's so funny?"

"The shifting lights."

For a second, she just scrunches her nose at me. And then it's like a light flicks in her mind. "Oh. You mean the traffic lights."

Nodding, I continue, "In Alkira, green is a sign of life while red is death."

"I've never heard of Alkira before. Is it far?"

"Very."

"You're not much of a talker, are you?"

"Not much to say."

We lapse into silence, the lights flickering past.

"My name is Katie, by the way."

Shifting in my seat I take a moment to properly look at Katie. Her red hair falls in waves down her back, half of it shaved around the ear. A metal wing rises from the bottom corner of her ear and up the side. Her arms are bare of any adornments, but her shirt hints at skin beneath, the lace flowers teasing my eyes.

Blinking, I shift back in my seat, covertly adjusting myself.

"That thing is still following us."

A quick glance in the side mirror confirms my fear.

"We need to be moving faster."

"Yah, well, I'm not getting a ticket. Just wait until we get on the highway."

Nodding, I try to focus on the last few minutes. To think not an hour ago I was shoveling down dinner, trying to make sure I wasn't late for work. Kian hadn't been to ecstatic to leave me at home, but I needed the money. The Councillors had decided that mom no longer needed as much support. That it was long enough now for her to be over the grief and moving on with her life. Except she hasn't.

I had hoped to get in a couple weeks of work in before the Shade came back. Get a few payments out of the way. But that all would have to wait.

There is no use worrying about it now. All that matters is getting as much space and time in between me and the Shade. Then and only then can I slip back to Alkira.

The threads taunt me, whipping past, begging me to pull on them and leave the Shade behind. But I know better than to accept that. That's how all the others died. Slipping through the threads too often only makes the Shade more in tune with you and your mark in the weave.

Last time, I waited two weeks on another world. I thought that long enough. But with the quick appearance of the Shade in Alkira, I'm second guessing myself. I'll have to stay longer on Earth before shifting back home.

Glancing over at Katie, I can't help but wonder as to why she is out so late at night.

"So..." she finally breaks the silence. Then the *click, click* of the blinker echoes through the car. I wait for her to turn the car and merge onto the main road. The highway as she called it.

"**So**."

CHAPTER 2

¢

The soft strains of a violin fill the space, mournful and angry. A voice joins it, and I cringe at the strange twang to his words.

Katie leans forward and dials the noise down, saving my bleeding ears.

"Can you tell me what that, that *thing* was?"

I have to tread carefully. Not that I know too much about the Shade myself.

"It's called a Shade. It hunts people."

"Yah, I got that. But why have I never seen or heard it before? I mean it came right out of the bush!"

Fingers tap to the beat of the song on their own violation.

"It hunts only certain people."

She waits, as if to give me time to elaborate. But there is nothing more to say right now.

Instead, I ask, "How does a car work?"

Katie looks at me, smirking before returning her gaze to the road again.

"Tell yah what, Jared, I'll tell you all I know about cars." I lean forward. "But under one condition."

"No."

"You haven't even heard what I have to say yet."

"Still no." I lean back in the comfy seat, crossing my arms.

We drive in silence for I don't know how long. The few lights from Ponoka long behind us. The occasional car on a road to the left of us lights up the night with a flash before returning the view to darkness.

It's so dark here. I can't remember a time that it was truly dark back home in Vert. It helps that we have three moons. Masa, Dlasa, and fAA. The first two are named after the great mother and father. The third, fAA, is not always visible. It is half the size of the other two. But every so often in our history it lights up a bright fiery red. The Story Keepers have no answer as to why it happens. Just that it does.

"Fine. I was going to say I'll tell you about cars if you tell me something about where you are from."

The light of the dash makes a ghostly mask over Katie's face. For a second, I'm reminded of someone else. Before I can catch on to the memory, Katie is turning to me, and I'm caught by her big glowing eyes.

"In Alkira, we don't have cars. But we do have hovers for moving small things. Most people just walk, only the old or the sick take hovers. The norms take the train."

"Wait, so you have trains, but you don't have cars?"

I nod, forgetting she can't quite see me.

"Yes."

"Weird."

I just say nothing. Sometimes it's better to say nothing at all. Silence can be power. Or so my dad always said.

Another crooning song comes on, this one a bit faster than the last.

"Well, you answered my question, now it's only fair I answer yours. To tell you the truth I don't know much about cars. They have an engine, where you have to make sure it has oil or the pistons will seize. Also, you need transmission oil, wiper fluid, steering oil, and a battery and car starter to start it. Does any of this make sense so far?"

"You'll have to show me the engine and then I'd probably understand it."

"Wait! I have a better idea!" She shuffles in her seat feeling up her pockets and down the side of the seat. I brace myself as we slowly swerve into the lane beside us.

"Found it!"

In her hand is a little box with a glass screen. Touching some buttons, it lights up and I watch in shock as she fiddles with the screen and still manages to drive in a straight line.

"Are you supposed to be doing that?"

"I'm a good driver. Don't worry about it." Dubious of the fact, I remain braced for impact. A quick glance in the mirror reassures me that at least we are ahead of the monster. I can't even make out a flicker of movement in the darkness behind us.

"Here." She shoves the flat box in my face. I hold it gingerly in my hands, just staring. It's much heavier than I expected.

"Touch the triangle and it will play the video. If you want to look up something else just go and touch the magnifying glass and type in what you want to search."

Daintily touching the triangle, I jump a little as the video begins. At first it throws me off that I can't pull it out of the screen. Apparently, earth's tech is slower in coming to age as Alkira's has already passed to holo's. Despite it, in seconds I'm engrossed by the video as it shows me how a V8 engine works. After the first video, I go and use the search like Katie and look up the difference between V8 and a V6.

From there I'm not sure how many pages I read or videos I

watch, but the next thing I know streetlights are appearing on the road again. In a daze, I ask Katie, "Where are we?"

"Red deer. I'll probably fill up in Gasoline Alley. Then I need to know where we are going."

"How much farther is it?"

"Another fifteen minutes. You may as well keep watching that video."

I grin sheepishly at her, turning back to the device in my hand. The device itself is simple. I shift my sight and look behind the glass, finding bits pulsing energy and metal gears. Now gears I understand.

I shake my head to straighten my sight again and pull up a video on planes. They are very archaic compared to the hovers we use now. Maybe, if I'm here long enough, I'll be able to go on one of these archaic machines.

Before I realize it, the car is pulling off from the main road and pulls into a brightly lit pad. The building behind is dark. Katie doesn't seem to be worried, pulling out a card from her pocket before getting out of the car.

Opening the door, I inhale a deep breath. The air is cool but not quite cold. I can't help but cough at the smell.

"Careful. The smog's pretty bad at night. Especially this last year, what with all these new people moving to the city." With more people comes more smells and a certain level of dirty that no matter how often I clean the front porch, still seems to hang.

I nod leaning back against the car. Katie pushes back a stray hair behind her ear before pulling the pump. It makes a hum, and I watch as the numbers rise on the screen in front of us. The reliance on fuel is what drove Alkira into a new revolution of motion, setting up our four great cities. But the land in ancient times had been riddled with villages. Or so Dad said.

Click.

Settling the nozzle back in its holder, she walks around the car and leans against the door, her arms stretching over the roof.

"So... where are we headed to?"

I shrug.

"Do you have any friends or relatives you can stay with?"

I shake my head at that.

Katie sighs.

"Do you at least have a credit card so you can stay in a hotel?"

"What's a credit card?"

Her eyebrows rise in disbelief, and she throws up her hands as if giving up.

"You have got to be kidding me," she mutters to the open sky.

I look down at my hands. They are calloused and rough from work, a bit scratched up and dirty from the forest. But these hands have gotten me through tougher times than this.

"Katie."

She pushes up her bangs before turning to me, one hand braced on her hip.

"Thanks. I can take it from here."

"Fuck that."

I jerk back.

"You don't have a credit card, probably no money, no one to contact. And you don't even know what a smartphone is!" I glance around the empty lot to see if anyone can hear her tirade. No movement. Turning back, I warily take in Katie's form as she huff's out a breath, looking up at the orange tinted night sky.

"Calgary." She nods to herself before turning to me.

"We'll go head to Calgary. It's about another hour and half driving to the city limit, and about a half hour to my aunt's place." I nod slowly, she continues, "She's really nice and probably won't ask to many questions if we show up in the middle of the night." Nodding to herself again, it's decided. Katie gets in the car and starts it without hesitation. I scramble to get in the car and barely get the door closed before she's already pulling out of the lot. We pass by brightly lit buildings in all different shapes. One looks like the mills of the east. I doubt it's a functional mill though.

Eventually Katie merges the car back on to the main highway and we are speeding along through the dark night. Nothing more than a streak. A flash of light that is quickly swallowed up and forgotten.

Katie reaches out to the volume button and turns it up. A woman is singing this time, her voice clear and quivering with power. Katie hums along.

"She has a beautiful voice."

For a moment she looks at me, her hum dying mid song.

"Not too many guys I know like Dolly Parton."

Shrugging, I just lean my head back and close my eyes, letting Dolly croon to me about Jolene.

"I didn't think you liked country with the way you were wincing to Ian Tyson earlier."

"Country is a place, that noise earlier was just that. Noise."

"Actually, that *noise* was a big hit in the seventies. And *A* country is a place, but *country* is a style. It can be a style of music, clothes, or even home décor."

"Whatever."

She just humphs, turning up Dolly Parton to the point of painful. I say nothing. At least this way I don't have to try and make conversation with her. Turning my head to the window, I

let my mind wander as the songs
blend from one into the other.

CHAPTER 3

¢

Calgary. Ten kilometers.

"Now we just got to survive the Deerfoot and then we'll be good to go."

I just shrug, not even bothering asking about what Deerfoot is. My eyes feely gritty with tiredness. But the digital clock on the dash says its only four in the morning. Makes sense. I was awake on Alkira from five thirty in the morning to when I left which was around four in the second sun. I've probably been awake for over twelve hours.

The light poles pass us by, lighting up the city in a fake morning. Katie turns us down streets lined with house after house that seem to have gotten stuck in a mirror. All of them are the same in colour, shape, and front lawns.

Katie slows down in front of one of these mirror houses, pulling the car to a full stop and wrenching the park brake on.

"Well, we made it. Hopefully someone's home."

It looks doubtful. The house does not have a single light on. The slammed door from Katie's side pushes me into action as I scramble to catch up to her. I slow down and match my pace with hers. We walk up the sparsely painted front porch.

Knock, knock, knock.

We stand there in silence. The porch has no decorations or even a chair to sit on. The lawns on either side of the house are meticulously kept, yet Katie's aunt's place is shaggy looking.

"Wake the fuck up, Terry," she mutters under her breath, bringing her fist up to slam on the door again.

Bang, bang, bang.

I watch as Katie starts pacing back and forth. Suddenly she stops and looks up at me, her mouth gaping.

"Shit!" she whispers as she covers her mouth with one hand and the other runs through her hair.

"How the fuck did I forget?"

"What's wrong?"

She turns to me, her face barely illuminated from the streetlights.

"My aunt is in Montana for the week on a business trip."

I scrunch my brows as I look down at her pale face.

"Isn't there another way to get in? Maybe a spare key?"

I watch as a light goes on in her eyes and she turns and scrambles down and around the porch.

"I've got it," she whisper screams. I don't think it would have made a difference to the neighbours since her knocks should have woken them up a lot earlier.

She skips back up the stairs and jams the key into the door, rattling it until I hear a click. Her eyes glint in the early morning light as she grins up at me with mischief. Katie brings up her finger to her mouth to shush me as she carefully opens the door. I step in behind her. She closes the door and goes to a beeping box on the wall beside. I take in the dark hall that is sporadically lit by the flashing light. After a couple moments she closes the box and quietens.

"Alright, let's get some sleep."

A loud gurgle stops her from taking another step. She looks back at me and I blush as my stomach lets out another deep groan, like a dying mosna.

"Or not." She turns and walks into a different entry, flicking lights on as she walks.

We enter a kitchen that is similar to the one in my own home. There are a few things that look a little different, the strange metal box with two slices on its top being one.

Katie ignores me and starts opening drawers. I'd offer to help but I have no idea what she is hunting for. Instead, I go to the small island and sit on the tall chair and watch.

"Aha!" She pulls out a blue box as if it is a great treasure, the Icsas incarnate.

"Prepare yourself, my friend, for food of the gods."

I snort at her exaggeration and watch as she pulls out a pot and fills it from the sink. As she sets it on the stove, she turns to the large metal cupboard and opens it. My eyes widen as I feel a cold breeze coming from its inside. A refrigerator. I'd only ever heard of them. They are more common in the east, where the technology base is far behind from us in Vert. I planned to move there, once I'm done school next month, maybe apprentice under one of the tinkers. Or Raul himself. He is like a god, I mean he *had* invented some of our major technologies on Alkira, such as the book printer, which can reprint the old manuscripts from before the 2nd Age.

My eyes zone back into the bottle Katie is holding out to me.

"Cheers," she says as she lightly clinks her bottle to mine before taking a large swig from it. I take a sip as well, hesitantly. The flavor reminds me of oranges, but bubbly and much sweeter.

Katie bursts out in giggles and I turn to her, making a face.

"Sorry. It's just your face, priceless." She giggles a bit longer before taking another swig, leaning her hip against the island, an eye on the pot.

"What is this?"

"Cream soda. I'd have offered you something better, like a cola, but my aunt is pretty weird and only buys this stuff."

I nod, taking another sip, a larger one. The bubbles seem to come right back up and I let out a loud burp.

"Nice one."

Then she lets out a burp, a bit longer than mine.

"Not too bad."

She winks at me. "Got to practice to impress the boys."

I snort mid swig, and soda comes shooting out of my nose, burning my nostrils. Katie takes me in and falls over laughing as I am chocking slightly, still laughing at her comment.

I don't know how long we are like that, laughing for no real reason. The long night, and long morning seems to have gotten the better of both of us. Katie gets up and throws a dishtowel at me.

"Thanks."

"No problem."

Wiping my face off, I walk over to the sink. I reach out and pull up, water spraying out at me, cool as a glacier spring. Cupping my hands, I clean up my face as best I can.

Then I wash out the towel and turn back and clean off the island.

For a moment I bump into her hip, and we are standing face to face. She stands just barely shorter than me. I'd just have to lean down, and her lips would be right there. Her eyes widen a touch. I glance down even farther and watch her tongue dart out and wet her lips.

And then I step back. What the hell. I mean, I think she is a very attractive girl. But I have Kian. And that's all I need.

Not to mention she's from a different universe than me...

Chucking the towel, it hits the tap and turns it off. I walk back around the island, keeping the cool granite between us.

She clears her throat and pulls a wooden spoon out of a drawer before pouring the contents of the box into the water.

"Should be another couple of minutes before its done." She opens and pours in a second box.

I sit there in silence and just watch as Katie stirs the pot occasionally, before pouring out the water. Then in a flurry of activity she's pours two packets of yellow stuff and some milk from a clear jug into the pot and stirs it all.

"You want hot dogs in yours?"

She looks at me for only a second before turning away and pulling some sausages out of the fridge and throwing them into a metal box with a spotted window. I watch as the sausages slowly turn, squealing as they heat up to the point of bursting.

Katie takes them out and cuts them up, adding them to the pot, deciding for me apparently. She divides the food into two large bowls and sets one in front of me with a spoon.

"*Bon Appetit.*"

"Uh, likewise?"

She smirks before pulling something out of the fridge and joining me at the island.

I take a hesitant bite of the noodles. An explosion of cream cheese, salt, crunch, and a fatty pork sausage fills my mouth. I moan in pleasure.

Pausing for a moment after shoveling half the bowl into my ravenous mouth, I turn to Katie.

"What is this?"

For a moment I'm caught up by her soft lips wrapping around the spoon.

She covers her mouth daintily with her hand before turning to me. I jerk my gaze away from her mouth and look up into her eyes instead.

"It's **KD**, you like it?"

"Love it."

She smiles and we don't say another word, just eating our late supper—or is it early breakfast?—in silence. Comfortable silence.

When I'm done, I walk over to the sink and with the rag there and the water running, I quickly wash my dishes off.

"Here."

I take her bowl as well and clean it. She pulls out a towel from somewhere and starts drying everything. With the last glass cleaned and the sink wiped down I glance at the clock. 5:22 am.

"May as well get to bed. Auntie has a couple spare bedrooms for visitors."

I nod and follow her out of the kitchen and up the stairs. She points to the second door on the right. "This one's yours." She keeps walking down the hall and turns into a room on the left. I look in the room she pointed out. Bed on the left, desk under the window, teddy bear on the floor.

I don't even look back as I keep walking, straight into Katie's room. For a second, I'm frozen by the view of Katie half undressed. A bra captures my attention. Finally, she gets her shirt off over her head and I avert my gaze before I'm caught.

"Fuck! Get out!"

I stay where I am. Shuffling noises try to pull my attention away from the window, but I stay stoic. I can see straight into the neighbour's house, which conveniently has a window at the same height, same spot on their house, except it is dark.

"What do you want, Jared?"

"Nothing."

"Then why the hell are you in here?"

I shrug. "It's safer if we stick together."

She walks in front of me and hands me some clothes. I raise an eyebrow.

"Pajamas, for you to sleep in. Unless you plan on wearing this to sleep in."

She looks me up and down, and I notice her interest. At least I'm not the only one affected here. May as well give her a show. I drop the clothes in front of me on the ground. Then I slowly pull my shirt over my head and drop it. For a moment her eyes widen as she stares at my chest. Kian always loved running his hands all over my abs.

She looks away before walking over to her bed and clambering underneath the covers.

"Goodnight," she mumbles from her blanketed nest.

I stare at the unmoving pile for a moment longer before shucking my pants and slipping on the clothes Katie gave me. Grimacing, I hold in a retort. Baby blue fuzzy bottoms with big pink and purple unicorns all over it. The shirt is at least just a plain black V-neck. A little tight. The pants are on the short side as well.

I get the feeling that these are her clothes. The thought warms me as I fold up my clothes and set them under the window, using them as a pillow. The lights from outside illuminate the room in perfect detail. The little princess crown on the bookshelf filled with stuffed unicorns in all shapes and sizes. A rocking horse at the foot of her bed.

It doesn't take long for the day to catch up with me. The last thing I notice is a light-weight pulled over me and then I'm out.

CHAPTER 4

¢

Cold fingers scratch up my chest, ticking away like little mice claws. *Aljariande Kar Vemesslschin.*

I can't open my eyes. I try to scream but something has my voice in a strangle hand. I go to push the fingers away, but a strange weight holds me down.

Feeling the creature pull up and back, its long silvery tentacled claws flash, I squirm harder against my invisible chains.

For breaking the laws of the universe, you will pay the price.

Before its greasy claw breaks through the skin on my chest I jerk up from the ground.

Breathing heavily, I'm lost for a moment. Going to class. Telling Kian to go home. The Shade finding me in the street. Running. Katie. I jerk my head to where her bed is. A mumble rises from her bed. Good. She's safe.

I stand up, wiping the sweat from my face onto my shirt. "Whew. Just a dream, Jared. Just a dream," I say to myself, trying to comfort my conscious and slow down my rapid heartbeat.

Turning, I run a hand through my short hair. For a second, I think I'm still in my dream.

A big red eye takes up the top half of the window. Then it blinks.

"Shit!"

Katie jerks up. "What?"

"It's here. No time."

I run over to the bed and pick her up, blanket and all, and run for the hall. The ominous screech of claws on glass permeates the air. The hairs on my arms and the back of my neck rise.

"What's going on? Put me down!"

"Can't. Shade. Here. Car." I'm panting as I run down the stairs, barely catching myself from tripping and falling the rest of the way down.

"Counter!" She yells pointing to the keys from the house and the other keys, which I assume are from the car. I grab both on my way by to the front door.

I'm already halfway down the front steps when she's yelling in my ear again.

"We have to lock the door!"

I ignore her and keep running for the car, dropping her to her legs on the driver side, before shoving the car keys in her hand.

"Get it started."

She opens her mouth as if to reply but I don't let her, vaulting over the front of the car and racing up the steps once more.

I'm shoving the key in the front door, swearing under my breath. I can feel the Shade moving inside the house. Don't ask me how because I can't explain it. Not to myself, not to anyone.

As I hear the click of the lock, the door shudders from the weight of the Shade running into it.

I drop the keys, "Fuck it," and run for the car. Thankfully Katie's inside and the engine is purring rather than coughing.

As I slam the car door behind me, halfway in the seat, I'm yelling, "Go. Go. Go." She doesn't even blink, hitting the gas and we screech around the corner, tires spinning.

"Watch out!"

Katie swerves, just barely missing an oncoming car. The loud horn beep behind us lets us know we were noticed. Not enough time to feel bad.

"Here!" Her phone slips through my finger and clatters around the foot rests. I duck and make a grab for it. Suddenly my head slams into the dash.

"Ow!"

"Sorry, pothole."

Rubbing my sore head and I turn on the phone.

"What's your password?"

"fifty-two. Eighty."

Typing it in, the phone glows before going to the home screen.

"Open up Google maps."

"What is that?"

"Never mind, grab the wheel."

She snatches her phone out of my hand and for a moment we are careening down a quiet residential road with no one on the wheel. I lean over the gear stick and grab on to the wheel, straightening us out. To my horror I watch as a little old lady is halfway cross the road.

"Brakes! Brakes!"

She jerks the car, and we just come to a stop inches away from the woman. She looks up at us with her milky gaze before continuing at her slow speed.

Katie shoves me back into my seat and hands me the phone again.

"Get your seatbelt on."

I'm just reaching for it when she's already slamming on the gas again. Once the buckle is in place I look to her for her next instructions. Instead, a cold voice speaks up. "In 200 meters, turn right."

And so Katie does. The cold voice from the phone navigates us through the bustling city streets and narrow one ways of the city of Calgary. I feel like I am taking a museum tour from the old city in Vert, flying through on my hover.

Finally, we get to a freeway. Our breathing has slowed, and the silence becomes deafening in the small car.

I look out the window as we cross over a bridge. The water underneath rushes past, not worried about anything stopping it. As timeless as the first world. And as mysterious. I can't help but smile as the afternoon sun bounces off the water, making it sparkle and dance as it crashes forward, always forward.

"So."

Turning, I take in Katie's rigid frame. Her mouth is just a slit.

"What the fuck happened back there?"

I'm not totally sure myself. I woke up from my dream just in time to notice the Shade. Something tickles at the back of mind. *Punished.* Yet I can't seem to grasp on to anything.

"The Shade found us."

"No shit."

"You don't have to be so mouthy all the time, you know that?"

She just sticks her tongue out at me.

Crossing my arms, I settle into my seat and stare forward at the winding road filled with other vehicles. Where were they all going? Where did they all start?

I hear a sigh. "Fine. I'm sorry."

I keep waiting, looking at her from the corner of my eye. She pushes out her bottom lip and bites it in worry. I shimmy in my seat.

"It's just, that was really close."

"We got lucky."

She nods.

With nothing else to say, we drive a bit longer in silence.

"I'll text my aunt about the house. So she's not worried about someone breaking in."

A building with a big yellow **M** passes us. My stomach grumbles.

Katie giggles. "I could go for some breakfast. Or late lunch," she amends looking down at the clock. It's more like evening. Twelve past four.

"Timmie's good for you?"

I just nod. It never stops to amaze me at how much Otherworlders from other universes assume a stranger should know or understand. I don't blame Katie for her. It just is.

She pulls the car into a turning lane, and we just squeeze around the corner before the flashing green arrow turns red. In mere moments Katie has us pulled into a line-up of cars. I watch as the line slowly inches forward. We pass a sign that states "drive-through". Interesting.

"So, what do you want?"

I look up at her with a blank stare.

"Right. Keep forgetting you're not from here. You like coffee?"

I nod. Her nose scrunches in distaste and I worry I made a mistake.

"Do you take cream and sugar in your coffee?"

She inches forward a bit and cranks her window down. A waft of bacon and eggs comes in and fills the car.

"Yes."

"Hi. Welcome to Tim Hortons. How can I help you?"

She turns to the sign that holds a big menu complete with pictures of various foods.

"Hi, I'll have a large hot chocolate and a large double, double. And two breakfast biscuit combos." She looks over at me for a moment before turning back. "Make that three."

"Alright. We'll have that ready for you at the window."

"Thank you."

She pulls up a little farther in the line. Then she turns to the middle console. She grabs for something but comes up with nothing but air.

"Shit." She starts scrambling through the centre console, before turning and looking in the back seats.

"What is it?"

"We forgot my wallet! It was right by my keys."

I'm not sure why it matters. And then it hits me. We probably have to exchange something in order to get the food. Not like back home, where you are given a card and you are marked off every time you use it, its max dependent on what kind of job you have. Tinker gets quite a bit of allowance since it is hard physical work.

"Thank god!"

I look over to see her pull out a unicorn pouch.

She pulls ahead and then we are by the window. A young girl in a uniform hands us a paper bag, which Katie promptly drops on my lap. She takes the two drinks and places them in the spot where her phone sat a moment ago.

Katie counts out coins of different colours and sizes before handing them to the lady.

"Have a nice day." The girl waves at us.

"You to," Katie gets out before cranking up the window and driving forward at the same time. I just sit and wait. She is able to wind her way back on to the main road before she turns to me.

"Man, we got lucky. I had just enough change for all this."

I nod.

"Your coffee is in the cup holder beside you. Want to hand me a sandwich?" She holds out her one hand, eyes on the road.

Opening up the paper bag I'm assaulted by the smell of bacon, grease. *Heaven.* I wade through and pull out a wrapped package. I half unwrap it before handing it to Katie's waiting hand.

"Thanks," she says before ripping out a big bite from the sandwich. My stomach grumbles again and I focus back on the bag and eat my own sandwich. I finish mine before her.

"The second one is for you." I smile at her before going for the second one. The sandwiches are absolutely delicious. I think I'll try making something like them when I get back home. Kian will hate them. He doesn't like to eat anything fatty or greasy.

"Want to pass me one of the hash browns?"

Passing it, I take out the other two for myself. I stuff all the papers, Katie's and mine, back into the paper bag. Then let out a loud burp.

She laughs.

"That was delicious. You all seem to really know how to make good food."

"I'm pretty sure your just easy to please," she teases me, lightly punching my shoulder. I can't help but grin.

"Probably."

"So."

"So."

"Where to next, since we can't go back to my aunt's place?"

I'm trying to think, but I don't know the landscape of earth well enough.

"Is there any place cold here? Like really cold, with snow and stuff."

"Like the mountains? Why?"

"I found out last time that the Shade doesn't really like cold, and it moves a lot slower in it."

She nods slowly. "Okay, we could probably make it to Jasper. But it's going to be another few hours driving again."

"Got nothing better to do here."

Katie smirks at me before leaning forward and cranking up the country music. I stick my tongue out at her, and we laugh as we pass the city limit. Despite being in a car, in a strange world, with a stranger, I've never felt so comfortable.

And peeking over at Katie, and her relaxed shoulders, she must feel it to.

Why is she helping you though? That is what I don't understand. But I shove the question out of my mind. There is no time for that kind of worrying. Right now, the only thing I need to worry about is surviving. For two weeks. At least...

CHAPTER 5

¢

I wake up with a start, looking for the source. Turning I see Katie with a sheepish grin on her face.

"About time, sleeping beauty, we are almost here."

Rubbing my eyes, I finally look outside for the first time since the Calgary city limits. I am awestruck by what I see.

"Is this Jasper?" I ask her as I stare at the great hulking teeth of the land as they come up like a craggy mouth.

"Not quite, these are the Rockies, Banff is a city farther into the mountains, and north of it, where we want to go since its nice and cold, is Jasper."

"A fitting name." The Rockies. Upon closer inspection I notice the bare tops filled with snow and scraggly looking trees.

"We should be there passing Banff in a half hour or so."

A beep distracts us both. Katie grabs her phone and looks at it before putting it down again, a frown marring her face.

"What is it?"

She hesitates for a moment, biting her lip. I lick my own unconsciously.

"It's my mom. She was wondering where I was." For a second, I'm confused and then I remember my earlier question.

"And what did you say to her."

This time she turns to look me in the eye. "Well nothing, obviously." *Why?* I wonder again. *Why are you doing this for me?*

"You should tell her something."

She waves my answer off. "I know, I'll just text her later, when I'm not driving."

With that we sit in silence as the landscape surrounding the car evolves from rolling hills to gray looming mountains, and eventually to snow tipped hulking masses of earth.

I can't help but marvel at the road. There seems to be a silent and accepted rule of slow cars in the right and fast cars in the left. This becomes even more so the farther into the mountains we travel. Lining the side of the road are signs with all sorts of pictures. Some have moose, others have deer, creatures I recognize from the history books as living traditionally in the north. But I have never seen one in person. Vert is a great city far in the south, walled in to keep the wild out and the civilized in. It protects its citizens from animals as well as from wanderers. An important duty considering the harm and destruction that follows the wanderers.

And yet, my dad was allowed to live inside Vert's great walls for a time. I always wanted to ask my mom about it. But since the day my dad died, she has become a shell of herself. There is no soul reflecting out from her eyes. If I don't remind her to eat, she won't. My friends don't know any of this. Or the council.

Yes, the council knows *my mom* is in grieving, but I don't think they know that the day Dad died, my mom—or at least the mom I knew—died with him.

"What are you thinking about?"

Katie's voice distracts me from my thoughts and I'm grateful for it.

"Nothing."

She glances over at me, but I keep staring out the window.

"Alright then."

The momentary silence between us is broken by a loud gurgle. I rub my belly, but I know it isn't me. Katie's cheeks redden.

"Um, I think I have some food in my winter emergency box in the trunk. I'll just pull over in Canmore."

I nod. The winters in Vert are nothing like the northern and western regions of Sersian and Leassian. Ours are mild with the soft patter of rain for months. But the north? If the history books are to be trusted, the winters are harsh, spitting snow and ice for months leaving people stuck indoor for days on end.

Katie clicks the signal before turning off the highway. She turns the car and keeps driving until we stop in a quiet section of gravel with a large map at the far end of the space. She jumps out of her door without a word.

I scramble with my seatbelt trying to follow her.

"Here."

I take the bar from her before following her lead and sitting on the tail end of the car. We munch in silence for a moment.

"So...how old are you?"

I look over at her, but she keeps watching the cars pass by below us. As if she hadn't asked me a question.

"Seventeen. Why?"

"Just wondering." She turns to me, her eyes wide with a small sparkle. "So where you're from, do they still make you do school?"

"What do you mean?"

Katie carefully tucks the wrapper into her jeans pocket but continues to sit on the tail. "I mean, here we have to do school from like age seven to like eighteen. After that you're an adult and can keep going to school or go to work or travel the world or whatever. But I have cousins, from overseas. They are finished school when they are fifteen. And I can't imagine it. I don't know what I'm going to do this summer, let alone three years ago." I track her hands as they fly through the air with quickening speed.

I'm not sure how to answer her, never having had to explain myself to an Otherworlder before. Normally I don't see people when I shift between the universes, or I try to avoid them or get away from them as best as I can. Besides this time with Katie, there has been only one other time where I had to explain myself.

A flash of black hair and my dad's eyes breaks through my thoughts before I can push the memories away. No. Not now. Not ever.

Shaking my head, I turn back to Katie who is watching me with rapt attention. I squirm on the hot metal for a moment before answering. "It depends on what region you are from. I'm from the south where kids normally go to school for half the week and work the other half until their nineteenth birthday."

Her eyebrows pull together as she mulls over my words.

"What makes the south different from the other places?"

"Um," I rub the back of my neck before continuing, "Well the north doesn't have as long summers to be out and work, so the kids have more time in school and are done by sixteen."

"Oh."

She turns back to the road, kicking her leg against the car light with a quiet thud.

"So, what do you guys do in school?"

"Math, history, language studies. Those are some of the basics everyone takes.

"Same here! Except we have social studies instead of history."

"What's the difference?"

She bites down on her thumbnail, chewing absently as she thinks.

"Well history just covers history where social studies teaches you how to think and understand the thinking of people in history. As well as learn about the history."

"They don't teach us to think in school."

"They should."

"Why? I already know how to think. I've been doing it all my life, like breathing. They can't teach me anything I can't already do."

"It isn't always a matter of doing, as it is a matter of

understanding. And they could totally teach you how to breathe, have you never heard of yoga?"

"What?"

"Exactly." Her eyes are lit with fire matching her burning hair. I've never seen someone so alive. And yet when she turns away, I can't help but think I've seen the curve of that nose before.

"You must be in high school then."

I jump off the trunk and stare at her. "How did you know?"

"I...uh...I guessed?" She shrinks back a bit from me. It takes me a moment to realize that even with her still sitting on the trunk I tower over her small frame and that's when it hits me. How I know her.

She is Rosa's seconder.

I'm frozen with shock as it all comes together. One of the few things known about the half-sighted, people who can see the threads of the other universes, is that it all started with the first world. Not much was found in the records of our world, the second world, except that we all lived as a mirror copy of the first world with one slight difference.

I never thought about it before, many of the worlds I fell into were unlike anything back on Alkira. And yet here, standing before me, I have proof that it is true.

Before I can continue on that same track with my thoughts, I grip my shoulder in pain. "Ow! What was that for?"

"For staring at me like some weirdo. Now come on. I'm over this. Let's get on the road. The sooner we get to Jasper the better."

Before I can say anything more she's gone in a whirl of red hair and flashing golden blues. I run to my door, barely slipping inside as she already backs it up. She has the radio cranked before I can say a word, letting me know that by no means does she want to talk to me.

Fine. I didn't want to talk to her either. I watch the mountains pass by and can't help but think I've stumbled across something important. Something that could change the very foundations of Alkira.

But I don't know if that's a good thing. Or very, very bad.

CHAPTER 6

¢

I can't help but stare as the great craggy beasts pass by the window. I've never seen anything like it. Or heard of it from Alkira's history books. Granted, our small school in Vert doesn't have access to the old tomes that hold most of our universes secrets. The Morsian have reprinted a few. But most were gifts, given to the printers by wanderers. Yet the four provinces fear the wanderers and do everything in their power to keep the wanderers and their kin out.

"Yah, they're pretty amazing," Katie breathes out on a sigh. When I glance over, I notice her relaxed shoulders and the glazed look in her eyes.

"They truly are. I've never seen anything like it."

"You don't live close to any mountains in your universe?"

"We don't have mountains on Alkira. Period."

"Oh..."

I shrug, not sure what to say. As the silence lengthens, I have an itch to fill it. As we pass the ice fields sign, I finally break down and talk.

"There are five main regions in Alkira. But the cities are only in four. My home is in the south, Karsian. It is very warm there. In the northern province, Sersian, there are fields of ice and hills of snow. But no mountains like here. To the east there is Morsian, and it is filled with warm rainforests. They say it's all green, year-round..."

For a moment I'm lost in the memories of bright holopics, completely surrounded by moss and leaves and grass. My fingers itch to reach out and touch. But I know better.

"You want to go there." Not a question.

"Yes." I turn to her, the ice reflecting light off her bright hair. "One day I will."

"Why haven't you already?"

"It's complicated."

She waits a few moments before replying, "Try me."

I take a few moments to stare at the snowcapped mountains and dark green forests that soften the edges. "There is only one way to travel from region to region. The DF collective. It is a single rail built after the fall of Rannor. It connects the four regions. But it is very hard to get a seat on it. Tickets are given by lottery to the general population. The council are the only ones who can buy a ticket for when they choose."

"I thought you said there are five regions..." She raised her brow at me, glancing away from the road.

"Well, there are. But the cities are in the four. The fifth, Valsion, is for the wanderers. It is in the middle of these four regions, a desert wasteland with no oasis or water to save a man."

"Yet people live there. These wanderers."

"Yeesss..."

"You don't sound so sure." She raises her brow glancing over at me. I shrug helplessly.

"The wanderers use to be the old inhabitants of Rannor. The great city was the only connection between the regions. All roads led to Rannor. When it fell, our world was left in an age of darkness. After many centuries the regions pulled together and built the DF collective."

"So, this city still exists?"

"There are legends about it. Many explorers have tried and failed to locate it. Most just disappear never to be heard from again. In my time it is against the law to apply for permission to search for Rannor. Instead, you are sent to rehabilitation in the north." I shiver at the thought. Rehabilitation is just another word for never to be seen again. Their names are forgotten, their memories lost. All that stayed was the surety that the council held the power to Alkira.

"Wouldn't the wanderers know where the city is? I mean you did say that is where they come from."

I'm shaking my head before she even finishes her thought. "The legends say that the city burned to the ground before being swallowed by the ground itself. There are eyewitness accounts in all of the regions that say that the city was lost. Besides, every piece of the desert has been mapped. There is nothing out there."

"Except living people." Her fingers tap subconsciously to the song on the radio as her lips are pursed in thought. "But people don't survive in the desert without some sort of source of food and water..."

"There is none. Besides the wanderers never live long."

"Why?"

"Because—*because* they just don't! I don't want to talk about it anymore." I turn myself to the window and watch with unseeing eyes as mountains and ice pass me by. She can't understand. The wanderers that roam the desert today aren't from the old city. They are kids, sometimes third or fourth generation, sometimes born by accident. The wanderers' genes linger in all of us, but for some reason a few are born with the gift. And as soon as the council finds and tests the child, they are sent to the desert with no care for the child's survival.

My dad's sunken in eyes haunt me. *Promise me, Aljariande, promise me.*

I shudder as I'm pulled into a memory.

The light filters through the window and lights up the living room. I play with my wooden blocks. Mom putters around the kitchen. I don't know why because we never have enough to eat. It's always the same three meals. Soup. Mash. Oatmeal.

I try to set the blocks into a building, red with white edges and a tall roof. I've seen them in the threads. I always wonder how big they are. There are never people around when I catch a glimpse through the threads, just a tall red building surrounded by flat fields.

Crash.

I stick my tongue out as I carefully balance the top blocks until I fit the key block at the top. There! Just like the glimpse. Giggling, I clap my hands.

"What do we have here?" With a scream, I'm thrown up into the air before a familiar pair of arms catches me and pulls me into a hug.

"Oomph! You've sure grown, my bug."

I smile up at my dad's face. His eyes sparkle the same bright green as mine. His familiar curling locks are down past his shoulders and his beard looks scruffy. The more I look, the more I see how much he's changed in the last month. There are lines between his eyebrows. A new scar winks at me from his cheek.

"Daddy?"

His eyes crinkle for a moment, the hunted look dissipating in the afternoon air.

"That's me. I'm your daddy. Now why don't you show your daddy what you built here?"

"Jarel, you should eat," my mom admonishes. I look over Dad's shoulder and see her standing in the doorway lit up like an angel. She keeps drying the already dry plate in her hand.

Dad turns and clucks. "Now Alani, I don't know how long I got." Her mouth tightens as her eyes shutter closed. With a sigh she turns and disappears back into the kitchen. Dad sighs to, gently bouncing me before sitting down in front of my block building.

I crawled out of his arms and grab some green blocks and start patterning them behind the red building.

"Where did you see this, Aljariande?" His sharp voice cracks through the air. Scared, I fall back on my butt and begin crying. Dad's pale face slowly fills up with colour again as he reaches out to me. I bat his hands away uselessly. He pulls me into his arms, gently rocking me.

"I'm sorry," he keeps whispering into my hair, a quiet prayer, "I'm sorry."

After a while my tears dry up and I loll back onto his shoulder, feeling sleep claw at my eyelids.

"Bug," he whispers my nickname this time. I glance up at him, nodding slowly. "Can you tell me where you saw this? It's very important for Daddy."

I nod again before toying with my sweater. Without glancing up, I mumble, "Through the threads."

For a moment his arms tighten around me, and I'm scared again. Before I can cry out, he relaxes, pulling my chin up to look into his eyes.

"I need you to promise me something, Bug."

I nod. Out of the corner of my eye I see the light darken a little in the window.

"Promise me you will never tell anyone what you see."

Again, I nod slowly.

"It's important, Bug, and when your older we'll talk about it, okay little man?"

Crash.

This time it is followed by Mom's scream.

"Shit!"

Dad drops me onto the ground, knocking over the red building.

"Daddy?" I cry out, my bottom lip trembling as I watch him disappear into the kitchen. Then another scream. Then quiet.

Too quiet.

Worried, I toddle over to the entrance and lean against the doorway. A quiet whimper pulls me farther into the darkened kitchen. There I find my mom hunched over on the floor, a small pool of blood at her feet. I crawl into her arms, worried by the deep gash on her arms. "Mommy?"

She shudders, still crying, silent now.

I want to ask her where Dad went but in my child's mind I

already know. Just like I always know never to touch the threads.

"Mommy?" I whisper again.

With a shudder, I'm blasted by the cold air from the climate control vents. I didn't agree with the council sending those kids into the desert. But I can see why. My childhood was filled with reasons why.

"Oh, I love this song!" Katie squeals out, reaching forward to turn up the radio.

I grimace. It sounds just like everything else that has played in an incessant drone. As I watch her bop and sing to the song my mind fills in the gaps. The dark bags that will form under her eyes. The gashes on her arms. The blank look, the only sign of a hollow body missing a soul.

If I'm not careful, if I am like my dad, that is exactly what will happen with Katie. With Kian. With anyone I let get close to me. Another shiver races down my spine. As I turn up the heating, I promise this girl who has helped me and asked for nothing in return; I promise her silently that I won't let that happen. I won't let the Shade get to her.

And I won't tell her who I really am. *What* I really am.

CHAPTER 7

¢

We keep driving up the quiet road, racing against the sun. As the evening light barely filters over through the mountains, I turn to Katie.

"Where are we sleeping tonight?"

Her eyes never stray from the road as her mouth tenses.

She lets out a sigh.

"Well, since we don't have my wallet, we can't exactly get a hotel."

"Is there nowhere else?"

She shoves her phone at me.

"There is the hostel, but I don't know if they will have any rooms left. Plus, we only have a couple of dollars in change. No. We will have to try something else."

I glance at the back seat of the car, noting its length and relatively comfortable looking cushions.

"Can't we just stop the car and sleep here?" I ask.

She frowns again.

"I don't exactly have a park pass, so technically we can't stay overnight in the park anyways. Plus, it's against park rules to sleep in your car on the side of the road. You could sleep in your car in a Walmart parking lot, or a campsite, but not the national park apparently."

Her eyes light up suddenly. I merely nod, not understanding much of what she said.

"That's it!" she shouts, smacking the wheel and accidentally honking the horn. Katie turns to me and playfully smacks my arm.

"Jasper is full of campsites. If we wait late enough, we could probably sneak in and not have to pay a camping fee."

With a grin, we continue down the road. I worry my lip, not sure about sneaking anywhere. I've never had much luck with sneaking in the past. Except for in the other universes, there it is necessary.

The sun continues to sink as we pull into the main street of Jasper. Both our stomachs rumble at the same time. I don't want to say anything. There is no more food in the car, and we can't afford to buy any.

Katie keeps driving, pulling into a small space. Before us stands a large building. The windows show people seated around tables, plates filled high with food around them. My stomach aches just watching them.

"Come on," Katie calls, already half out the door.

I scramble after her as she walks into the place. The woman at the front table stares at our clothes pointedly. Looking down, I realize I am still wearing the horrid unicorn pajamas. I glance away from her, my cheeks hot.

"A seat for two, please," Katie asks, staring the other woman down. The woman pauses before looking down at her clipboard. With a nod she begins walking away.

"Right this way," she calls over her shoulder.

Katie follows without hesitation, I stay a step behind Katie.

The woman puts us at a corner booth, farthest from the door. Katie sits down immediately. I follow suit.

"Your waitress will be right with you."

With a tight smile, she turns and almost runs back to her table at the front.

I turn to ask Katie what we are doing but she just shakes her head.

Another young woman comes by, similar dressed as the first. Before she can say anything, Katie is already ordering.

The woman scribbles furiously, trying to keep up with Katie before disappearing. All of it sounded like gibberish to me. But the breakfast was good, so I trust Katie with knowing good food. Not to mention the KD from the night before.

Katie turns to stare at the passersby on the busy night street. I take the moment just to watch her.

Her hair shines bright red, almost luminescent. It stands out against her too pale skin, popping out the few freckles speckled across her nose and cheeks. Despite her freckles, I can't help but notice the dark roots in her hair, almost brown.

Is it possible the red is not her true hair colour? If so, she was Sae's twin. While I never really took the time to look at Sae, having grown up as neighbours, and later becoming friends in primary school, I know she is pretty. If Kian didn't ask me out back when we were just fifteen and gangly, it might have been different. But now, I have eyes only for my man. Just as my mom has been faithful to dad, even after death, so too do I want to be with Kian. Though... We have disagreements. A lot, recently.

A lot, a lot, since the Shade started coming more regularly to my home.

Since I began to disappear for a month or two at a time.

It is hard to stay close when I am in a different universe. But my dad did it. I will to.

Blinking, I realize two steaming plates are sitting before me and Katie. That and she already has a mouthful of noodles in her mouth.

She wipes her mouth, not looking up at me. "Eat quick."

I don't question her and shovel back the creamy noodles, barely holding back another moan. Food here on Earth was nothing like Alkira. While our food back home was filling, it didn't really have any flavor. Probably because food processing, packing, and distributing has been centralized since the thirties. That and food is produced mainly in the south and the east.

I'm still shoveling food back when Katie gets up and disappears around a corner. I try not to worry, continuing to eat my food. By the time she makes it back to the table, I just finish the last bite of my meal.

She slides in across from me, opening a new menu.

"You should probably use the bathroom. Meet me in the car after."

Not once does she look up at me. A shiver runs up my neck, but I ignore the feeling, this time it has nothing to do with the Shade and everything to do with Katie's avoidance of looking at me.

Shrugging, I slide out of my booth and stumble around the room, following another man into a room with a simple stick figure on it. Strange.

I am used to bathroom's having the universal WC.

I just slide into the car when Katie comes hurrying down the sidewalk toward the car. She glances back once before pulling her door open.

"Don't ask," she cuts me off before the words fall out of my mouth. I wrinkle my brow, watching as the first woman, the one who seated us, pulls open the door of the building.

Katie throws the car into reverse and pulls out of there full speed.

She doesn't slow down until the city lights of Jasper are behind us.

I don't ask what we both know just happened. And by the tense way Katie holds her shoulders, I realize this is not her normal either. I am asking too much of her.

I probably just got her in trouble in her universe.

After a beat of silence, I finally say something.

"Just drop me off here."

She glances over at me, the dash lighting up the confusion in her eyes.

"I didn't mean to get you in any trouble. Shit, I haven't been thinking at all since I fell into Earth. I just—I just don't want you to suffer because of me."

Another beat of silence.

She turns stiffly to the road, driving, before finally responding. "It's too late now."

"It doesn't have to be. Just drop me off now. I'll stay low for a couple days—"

"No."

I'm shocked at her immediate answer. I look over and see Katie is shaking, her knuckles white as she clenches the steering wheel.

She continues in a slow voice, her jaw clenched. "I don't know what's going on but whatever that

thing is, it means business. And—
" She hesitates, glancing over at
me as her cheeks flush. "And if I
left you now, I'd be left the rest
of my life wondering what
happened to you."

My chest is warm at the
realization that she cares enough
to worry about me. Me. A
complete stranger who has been
nothing but trouble.

"Thanks," I mumble and stare
out the window.

We drive in silence for a couple
of minutes, twin lights from our
car lighting up the road.

Soon Katie slows, squinting over
the wheel. "I think it's this one..."
She mumbles as she bites down
on her lip.

I just watch.

She slows the car down, and
before we turn, she hits the
lights and lowers our windows.

The brisk evening air chills me instantly. I rub my arms. Hopefully its cold enough to slow down the Shade.

The gravel crunches beneath the tire as Katie steers us through the blackness of the trees. Finally, she pulls into a spot off the main trail into a dead end. She rolls the windows up and turns the ignition.

The silence is immediate. It weighs down on both of us. I look out the window, not sure what will happen if I look at Katie.

"I think I have a blanket in the back," Katie whispers.

I nod.

She opens the door and disappears.

Not wanting to sit alone, I join her. She already has the trunk of the car open, pulling on something I can't see.

Before I can offer to help, she goes around to the back door and pulls the seats down. I do a double take. The mobility of the seats is amazing, and the inner tinker in me wants to know what other secrets are hidden in the machine.

"We... uh... We should probably sleep close, since they uh, car isn't insulated, and it'll get a lot colder." Katie tucks a hair behind her ear, glancing up at me before she climbs into the back of the car.

I hesitate. I've only ever shared a bed with my mom. Not even with my boyfriend, Kian. It seems very strange to have this first in my life with a girl, from a different universe.

Meanwhile, Katie crawls into the back and pulls a blanket and pillow out of the trunk. I stare at the single blanket.

Katie must have misread my look because she mumbles, "It's for my emergency kit. You never know..." Then she looks up at me. "Are you getting in?"

Jerking out of my thoughts, I nod. It takes some maneuvering to swing my legs in and shimmy down. I have to keep my legs bent to fit. My head is beside Katies. Staring at her rigid body as she faces the ceiling. The moonlight illuminates her pert nose, her high cheekbones.

She really is beautiful.

I turn back and slam the door closed behind me. Then I turn back to face her. Katies eyes are closed, her hands tight on the blanket at her chin. We lay there in silence.

I don't know how long I lie there, listening to her breath. But eventually she whispers, "I've never had a boyfriend before."

I open my eyes and find myself staring into her eyes, the moonlight making them glow.

She turns her whole body, until we face each other, our faces only a breath apart. And then she blows my mind.

"I've never even been kissed before."

For a long moment I stare at her lips, wondering what they will feel like. Will they be strong like Kian's? Or will they melt underneath mine.

Blinking, I look into her eyes. "I've never slept beside someone before," and then I add, looking away, "besides my mom."

Katie shuffles closer, tucking her head underneath my chin. I carefully lay an arm around her waist.

For long minutes, I lay there wondering if she will say anything else.

Then she sighs in her sleep.

My heart warms.

I close my eyes and join her.

CHAPTER 8

¢

Moonlight filters into the car. I move my hand to rub my eyes. And then freeze. Sometime in the night, I turned onto my back, and Katie rolled half onto me, our legs entwined, her arm around my bare middle.

Shit.

My skin tingles from the heat of her hand on the small of my waist. Her hot breaths puff out on my chest as her hair scratches my chin.

The heat of her body warms my soul. Reminds me of what I am missing. If I wasn't been this way, I would be back home in Alkira, spending my days tinkering and my nights laughing and cuddling with Kian.

My hand tightens on her waist, and I pull her a little closer.

Then again, this, right here, right now, feels pretty amazing to.

A muffled noise filters through the car windows.

Frowning, I turn my head and am met with a big black eye.

My heart skips a beat. I jerk upright.

Katie falls off my chest, shouting, "What—What is it? Shade?"

The bear stands on its back feet and roars at us.

I feel the blood leave my face as I push Katie behind me toward the opposite door. She yanks at the handle with no luck.

"Fucking child lock," she swears under her breath as the bear's front paws brace on the window, the claws screeching down the surface.

Katie pops the door open just as the bear rocks the car. The window cracks.

"Jared!" she whisper shouts, pulling at my arms. I turn and scramble out the passenger door, my legs getting tangled in the blanket as I fall in a heap to the ground.

Katie helps me up, one hand on the blanket the other in my hand as she pulls me away from the car.

I look back, the moonlight illuminating the huge creature as it falls to its feet and walks around to the other open door.

Katie jerks on my arm. "Come on!"

The bear swings his big head toward us.

I turn away and start to run. The trees blur past us as we stumble through the underbrush. Soon, I'm the one dragging Katie as my long legs easily step over logs and past branches.

"Slow down," she gasps out.

It's only when she breaks my grip from her hand, do I actually stop. Katie is bent over her knees, gasping. I'm sweating, the slight breeze in the night cooling my skin quickly.

She stands up and rubs her eyes.

Then she drops them quickly and looks to the sky. "Fuck!"

"What?" I ask, rubbing a hand through my hair as each twig breaking has me twitching.

"I left my phone back there!"

I slowly turn and its then both Katie and I realize our mistake. Her eyes widen even further as her whole body begins to shake. I quickly walk up to her and pull her into my arms, hugging her hard. "It's okay," I whisper even though I know it's a lie.

She falls apart, crying into my shirt, great sobs wracking her body. I rub her back, trying to soothe her, even as I'm panicking on what we can do next. Because we are lost in the woods, trees all around us, and no idea which way leads back to the campground.

Her sobs slow to hiccups until finally, she pulls out of my arms and rubs her face. Taking a deep breath, her shoulders fall low. She looks defeated.

This is all my fault. If I left from the very beginning, I wouldn't have dragged a total innocent into the disaster that is my life.

The threads tempt me, glistening with lights from cities and suns over beaches. One touch. One step. And I could be a universe away, safe and warm. But my gaze sharpens and takes in Katies pale face, the dark glint of red in her hair as the moon stays true over us.

Sighing, I rub my hand through my hair again. I have to fix this. I can't just leave her. Not when she has done so much for me. Has lost her car, her phone, and any connections to those who know her and love her and protect her.

My fist clenches around the blanket in my hand. With nothing else coming to mind, I walk to the closest tree, a thick elm. I start to gather some of the dried leaves at the bottom.

"What are you doing?" Katie asks in a quiet voice. I glance up to see her rubbing her arms as she watches me.

"Making a fire."

Her eyes widen. "But—But what if it goes out of control and we start a forest fire?"

I snort. "It will be fine. I've made fires before." I gather a few sticks and heap them together. The grass is still damp that I'm not worried about it growing too big. I reach into my boot and pull out the knife I always have on me.

Katie comes and kneels down beside me, watching anxiously as

I flip the knife and pull out the small steel match. I strike it a few times before the leaves start to smoke.

She opens her mouth to say something, but I interrupt her. "Wait here," I murmur as I get up to look for a few larger branches. Fire will keep the wildlife away. Or monsters.

Once I return with a few dried-out spruce branches, Katie is huddled close to the fire, her hands out, trying to gather its small warmth. She jumps when I came up beside her.

I silently stoke up the fire, carefully breaking and placing branches to increase the flame to a manageable size. Once its burning hot, I lean back against the elm trunk. Katie is still kneeling beside me, the blanket wrapped around her shoulders.

Sighing, I pat the ground between my legs. "Come here."

She looks at me, her teeth chattering loud enough that I can hear them. After a long pause, she takes a breath before crawling over and settling in my lap, curling into my chest.

I pull my knife out, unclipping the sharpener and slowly work the blade to a clean edge again.

Long minutes of silence pass, broken up by the crackles of the flames and the rustling of wind through the leaves. Katies shivering slowly subsides. She snuggles closer into my chest. I can feel myself stirring and try to think of other things besides the warm pliable body pressed up against me.

"Where did you learn to make a fire?" she whispers.

I thought she had fallen asleep. I answer her honestly, staring at the blade and sharpener in a trance. "A bushman. I never did find out what universe I was on at the time."

Her fingers swirl small designs against my stomach. I groan lightly at the sensation, my muscles tightening as my heartbeat picks up. "Do you know how many universes are out there?" She tries hard to sound casual, but I pick up the hint of worry and interest in her tone.

"No idea. I personally have been to just over two dozen." I hesitate, not sure how much I should say. I have stayed on other universes before, keeping outside of the contact of the people. This is the first time I've really talked to an Otherworlder, like really gotten to know them. But it feels good to finally talk about it to someone. I have spent my whole life hiding. And would it really matter if I tell her? I bite my lip before continuing in a slower voice. "I have seen hundreds more in the threads. Not all universes are hospitable to people. Some are nothing more than an ice planet. Or have giant monsters that have eaten all the people. It's tricky picking the right thread to a place that won't kill you."

Katie is quiet for a long while. I finally put the knife away and gently wrap my arms around her. There is something about this girl that makes me feel overly protective. More so than I ever felt for Kian.

"Can you take someone to another universe?" she whispers.

I stiffen.

I have never done it before. Not even brought anything with from another universe back into Alkira. Even the thought of it feels wrong on such a basic level. Take someone through the threads? The only person in my life who knows I can even see them is dead.

I'm sure my mom wonders but she shut out the world years ago.

And Kian?

I don't know. I've never told him. He never asked why I disappear. It has never come up before in the last few years of seeing each other. The last few weeks though...

Katie snuggles even deeper into my chest and sighs. My hand comes up and gently pats her hair, its length soft despite the curls. The movement soothing as much to me as it was to her.

Soon her breathing evens out and she snores softly, leaving me to my thoughts. And wondering, what happens if I take someone through the threads? It is unheard of. Not even the rumors of the half-sighted have ever mentioned an ability to take people with. Everything about the half-sighted is left in rumor and legend.

I stare at the flames, entranced by their dancing colours.

No. Even if I can take someone through the threads, I won't. It is dangerous. Going through the threads is the reason for why the Shade hunts me. And to leave an innocent who can't jump between universes to the Shade's mercy is wrong.

My arms tighten around Katie.

And I won't leave her until she is safe at home. Only then will I go back to Alkira.

CHAPTER 9

¢

Eventually, the sun cracks through the branches. My arms have fallen asleep hours ago, but I didn't want to wake Katie.

But now, with the cool morning sun warming my face, and the reminder that the Shade is still hunting me, I know it's time to move. And the first thing to do, is gather some breakfast.

I carefully untangle Katie from my arms. She settles noiselessly on the ground. I let myself stare at her for a long moment, just taking it all in. Her pale skin dotted with barely there freckles across her nose. Her mass of curls cushioning her face from the hard ground. A single red curl bouncing Infront of her nose, barely tickling her nose. She looks serene and beautiful. And something about her, something I can't seem to find a name for, tugs at the sight of her.

I take a deep breath, shaking my arms out as the pins and needles crawl up and down them. Then, I carefully push off the ground and stretch.

The forest is quiet from the sounds of humanity and awake with nature. Birds sing loudly from the tree branches as I tromp through the underbrush. Using the bottom of my shirt as a basket,

I collect only the familiar berries. Raspberries, strawberries. A dark blue berry that is surprisingly tart. There are a few red and white berries on bushes that look tempting, but if the birds aren't eating them, then I'm not touching them either.

My head aches from the lack of sleep, from limited water. At least I had a meal yesterday, I remind myself. At times like these it's hard to be positive. But I'm alive. The Shade is here on this universe and not at my mom's house. And I met a girl. An interesting one who is loud and kind.

I try to think if Katie is anything like Sae. I mean, her eyes are the same. Her face. But Sae doesn't have the same red hair.

I come up to a large swath of dark blue berries. Perfect. I settle in front of the first bush and pick methodically, my shirt filling up.

Maybe Katie coloured her hair, I muse. It doesn't explain the curls...

There is a simple answer to my questions. Ask Katie. And I will, I tell myself, when we aren't running for our lives. Maybe it is time to find a way back to Katie's home. With her safe, I can leave.

By the time I return to where we slept, Katie is sitting up against the tree, her eyes wide as she watches me approach.

"Morning." My voice comes out as growl, scratchy from no water or sleep.

She gives me a wan smile before focusing on my shirt. Her eyes brighten. "Is that food?"

I settle down beside her, careful to keep from spilling berries everywhere. Even now I can feel the cool drip of crushed berries on my abs. "Freshly picked from the forest," I quip.

She wrinkles her nose, quickly shoving her hands back under the blanket that is still wrapped around her.

With my free hand I pop a couple of the dark berries into my mouth. The flavor has grown on me in the last hour. "You should eat some," I say as I hold my shirt toward her.

She bites her lip as she stares at the dark berries.

I stop eating, distracted by the sight of her bottom lip, red and swollen from her teeth.

"I'm not a saskatoon fan," she mumbles, reaching out and grabbing a single dark berry. She pops it into her mouth. I can't help but stare at the flash of her tongue. And then she pops another berry in.

Her gaze shifts to mine. I quickly look down, my cheeks burning hot. I ask the first thing that comes to mind. "What are saskatoons?"

I shove another handful into my mouth before daring to look up into her wide golden blues. Her cheeks are slightly flushed, but she answers quickly. "Those dark berries you have. They grow really well in the wild here in Alberta."

I nod, pretending to understand what she's saying. In this way, Katie is as alien as all the people I've met in other universes. Completely certain of their own world, and oblivious of how much they take for granted in their own language.

We eat in silence, finishing off the berries. I look up and laugh at the red stains around Katies mouth.

She frowns, pushing my shoulder in annoyance.

I get up and stretch, ignoring the sticky wet front of my shirt. Beggars can't be choosers.

Katie carefully stands up, still clutching the blanket around her shoulders. Shivers wrack her body. She doesn't say anything, peering out into the surrounding bush as she worries her bottom lip. "What are the chances of a bathroom being close by?" she whispers.

At the same moment, a distant honk echoes through the trees. Katie and I both turn toward the direction it came from. "If the road is that way," I start.

Katie says nothing. She steps around me and starts walking with hurried focus. Her urgency to pee must outweigh her fear of bears and other wildlife.

I smile, shaking my head as I follow behind her.

For once the strange tickling sense in the back of my neck is quiet. The Shade isn't close by. We are safe from immediate danger.

Time passes as sweat drips down my face and soaks into the collar of my shirt. The entire shirt sticks uncomfortably to my skin. Katie has her blanket tied around her waist, her sleeves rolled up, sweat stains on her back and armpits.

The sound of traffic gets louder the farther we walk. Honks are intermingled with brakes, loud beats of music, and the occasional growl of something louder. All the noise is new for me. Alkira's technology is built for silence. Minimum vibrations that affect nature and our bodies the least.

But this universe doesn't have any such aversions.

Katie growls as a branch swings back and smacks her in the chest. I reach past her and hold it aside.

She looks up at me gratefully, tripping and catching herself in the next step.

When we both finally look up, I realize we have finally made it out of the trees. Ahead of us, going in either direction is a long stretch of road. And to our right is several small huts, a building with the smell of food, and lots of vehicles.

"Thank fuck," Katie breathes out as she stumbles and runs to the nearest small hut. By the time I walk up to the hut she disappeared in, Katie is already opening the door and wiping her hands with a strong smelling acid. I wrinkle my nose at it.

"All yours," she murmurs, walking a few steps away from the hut and staring out at the parking lot.

Inside, a distinct odor lingers in the air. When I lift the seat, I realize why. The toilet is simply a hole in the ground. No filters. No catcher system. No water.

I hold my breath as I quickly relieve myself. As soon as I put the lid down, I take a shallow breath. Turning, I see no water, just a small pump on a bottle. I take a tentative pump of the acid.

The scent is strong enough to burn through the lingering odor in the space. At least there is that.

I push the door open with my elbow. The moment I spread the acid, I hiss in pain as the small cuts from berry picking burn. Before I can comment, I hear Katie whisper, "I have an idea."

I look up and see where she's looking. My gaze lands on two wheels, a motor under the seat. At least twenty in a row.

"I don't know," but she's already walking toward the rows of motored bikes with purpose. I run to catch up to her, glancing around the otherwise quiet parking lot. No one is watching us.

Still.

She confidently walks past the first couple of motored bikes before stopping on a sleek black one. It looks too small to hold two people. But Katie smiles like she found a treasure. She fiddles with the seat and pulls out a helmet. She looks to me, biting her lip. "There's only one helmet..."

I glance at the bike beside me. I quickly find the latch in the seat and pull out another helmet. This one with goggles. I hold it up for her to see. Her eyes light up.

"Perfect! Let's get out of here," she says as she shoves the helmet over her head. I do the same.

Katie pushes the stand up and easily hops onto the bike. When the motor roars to life, I realize why she picked this bike. "Come on," she beckons, her eyes glittering behind the shield of her helmet.

I carefully slide on behind her. I don't know where to put my hands.

"Hold on tight!" she calls, revving the motor until it growls like a demon.

I wrap my arms around her waist and do as she says. A good thing, because in the next moment, we are leaping forward on the pavement. Katie leans and maneuvers the bike through the parking lot and onto the long winding road.

We fly along the road, the wind making it impossible to talk. All I can do is hold on tight and watch the blur of trees and other cars pass us.

Hours later, and the mountains long replaced with an unending stretch of forest, we finally pullover. At first, when Katie turns the motor off, I can still feel it rumbling through my ass. My fingers are stuck, still clutching her middle.

"You can let go no," Katie says, her voice scratchy.

I cough before admitting, "I can't. They're stuck."

She slowly pries my fingers apart. Once they release, I stumble off the back of the bike, almost falling flat on my face.

Katie, on the other hand, adjusts the bike to stand on its own and is making a beeline for the building.

I stretch my fingers out, trying to get control of my trembling body. Finally, I follow her into the building. Which hosts bathrooms. But these look a lot more like what I'm used to.

When I get outside again, Katie is already seated on the motored bike.

"We need to get going." Her eyes are wide, shoulders tense as she keeps glancing at the road we turned off.

I jump back on without another word. There were over a dozen bikes in that cement pad...

CHAPTER 10

¢

Another hour and we pass a large sign. Edmonton. Five Kilometers.

But with the sign came clouds. The setting sun disappears as thick rain clouds darkened the sky all around us. By the time we hit the city limit, the rain is driving down on us. I'm not sure anymore if I am shaking from the motor, the rain, or the cold.

Katie suddenly pulls off of the road. My legs tighten around hers as I almost crush her with my arms. I can't hear her. We bounce through the dirt, as she maneuvers the short hill.

And then the rain is gone.

Or more accurately, we are no longer in the rain.

This time when I stumble off of the back of the motored bike, I do collapse onto the ground, shivering.

Katie turns the bike off and for a moment the only sounds in the world is the patter of rain on the ground.

Then the swish of a car passing overhead.

I flip onto my back and look up.

We are under a bridge.

"We should be safe here until the rain passes. Then we can keep going after," Katie's voice sounds far away as it bounces through the relative darkness.

I grunt in answer, my eyes sliding closed as my body aches. The chills are slowly getting worse now that I am out of the wind.

I feel a warmth on my side, when I look down, I see Katie snuggled into my chest. "Do you think you can make a fire?" she whispers, her teeth chattering and her lips purple with cold.

"In a bit," I promise, wrapping my arms around her. In a bit when I am warmer. Steadier. But for now, all I can do is lie there and listen to the chatter of our teeth.

I rub her back hard, for the friction and to get the pins and needles out of my hands. Long minutes pass before my shaking subsides. It's then that I get a good look around us.

The section of bridge we are
under is a sand hill. Far below is
the river, rushing past. And to
the far side I can make out the
fuzzy shape of bushes. I gently
set Katie beside me. She curls
into herself, still shaking slightly.

"I'm going to start on that fire."
Before I do move, I glance back
at the bike. "What are the
chances that there was more than
just a helmet storage in the
bike?"

She turns to me, her eyes
brightening, before her gaze
slides past and focuses on the
motored bike.

Leaving Katie to search the
bike, I head to the bush. While
the rain is still coming down hard,
there is quite a bit of dry leaves
and twigs underneath the bridge.
I shove what I can into my

makeshift pocket from the front of my shirt.

By the time I return to Katie, she has a flask and a couple of silvery bags out. She grins at me as she rips the first one open. "I've never been so happy for caramelized peanuts."

She moans at the first bite, and my body jerks with awareness. God she is something else.

I look away and focus on building us a small fire.

Once its burning, I sit back. Katie settles beside me, our arms touching, as she wordlessly hands me the rest of the bag of peanuts. The flavor is earthy, yet sweet, and almost buttery. I'm reminded of NutDip from Morsian, the eastern province. Of my mom, on her good days, taking me to the marketplace. She would set me in front of the Morsian vendor and give me one token to use.

And then she would disappear for the morning.

I loved those days, talking to all the peoples from all the different cities. And hearing about the different technologies. It's what got me interested in tinkering.

"There are a couple of granola bars to. I wasn't sure if you wanted to eat them now or save them for later..." Katie eyes the bars hungrily. A part of me wants to wait, to be sure. But then, in all my years of running, it has always worked out one way or another.

I grab one of the bars. "May as well sleep with a full belly. I don't think the rain is letting up."

We both look out into the darkness. The shimmer of rain

flashes with fire light as we are surrounded by the inky night.

Katie grabs the other bar and rips into it. Her face pinches as she stares out into the night. I can't help but watch her face. The way the fire lights up her eyes, warms her skin.

Katie turns to me abruptly. "What?" she growls.

My cheeks hot, I turn away and rub my hand through my hair. "Nothing," I mutter. I keep my eyes on the fire as I mechanically eat the bar. Granola bar remind me of the serving my family was given when Dad was still alive. Tasteless, filling.

Katie squirms beside me, before leaning against my shoulder. Without thought, I wrap an arm around her waist. She sighs, snuggling into my collarbone.

My eyes are just starting to close when Katie says in a quiet voice, "you must get lonely, travelling universes by yourself."

My grip tightens. I force myself to relax and take a deep breath. "It's not bad. And I do have my mom and my friends to go home to every time."

When she doesn't say anything, I find myself opening up. About everything. Except for Kian.

I tell Katie about my mom and growing up without a dad. About my school years. And my mentor who took me on as an apprentice tinker. I tell her everything except about the boy who has been at the centre of my heart for so many years. Maybe it's the warmth of her body, or the way the fire flickers in her eyes, but I can't find the words to tell her about my best friend...My boyfriend...

Slowly her shivers dissipate. With the firelight flickering in front of us, we both fall into the magic of a story told before a flame with the darkness of night surrounding us. I almost forget that Katie is in my arms, so caught up in the happy memories am I.

When I finally fall silent, Katie is lying in my lap, her hand on my chest. The fire flickers, her bright red hair glinting with its own flame. Katie turns to look up at me. The moment feels heavy, with things said and unsaid. Her eyes flicker to my lips. Her tongue peeks out as she wets her own. I can't stop myself from staring. From wondering. From leaning forward.

From hesitating right before my lips touch hers.

We sit there, a breath apart, souls almost touching. Yet neither one of us moves.

She shivers in my arms, her eyes closed as she whispers, "There isn't a girlfriend waiting for you back home?"

I pull back, the words like cold water down my back.

Katie frowns as she blinks up at me. The space between us feels like miles rather than inches.

"Jared?"

I rub the back of my neck before finally looking her in the eye. "I only have two friends from school. And Sae is just a friend."

Katie's eyes narrow before she turns to face the fire again. She snuggles back against my chest, but I can still feel her rigid back. Her tense shoulders.

"Tell me about her," she finally asks, breaking the silence.

I feel equal parts relieved and guilty. I am being honest. Sae is a girl who is just a friend, and I have no girlfriend. But I know what Katie is really asking. If there is anyone waiting for me at home. And there is. Just not a girl.

So instead, I throw myself into talking about Sae, who I have always had an easy friendship with since school. "I've known Sae since we were kids. We've always been able to chat. And she lives just down the row from my house. We used to walk to and from school every day. We don't talk as much anymore, now that she's apprenticing to be a Knowledge Keeper."

Katie pulls my left hand from her waist and into her own hands. Tingles roll down my spine from her fingers intertwining with mine. I can't stop the shuddering breath that leaves me. Heat fills me, not all of it from the warmth of her body.

"Is she pretty?" Katie whispers.

I shrug. "I don't know."

She leans back against my shoulder and tilts her head to look up at me. Her brows are scrunched together.

I sigh and look into the fire as I reply. "I guess. I mean, she looks a lot like you. She's the same height, same eyes, and when you smile you look a lot like her.

"But instead of bright red hair, Sae has long brown hair that she always has back in a braid that goes past her waist. Does that answer your question?" I ask as I turn to look down at her.

Katie snorts. "A year ago, she would have been my doppelganger."

Now I'm the one frowning. "What do you mean?"

Katie sits up and turns in my arms, her legs over my left leg as her shoulder leans into my right shoulder. Once she's half facing me, she answers while moving her hands, "It's just that a year ago I cut my hair and got it dyed and permed. Before that I had never done anything with my hair except put it in a braid. I donated sixty centimeters to the Angel Hair foundation, I had that much."

Confused, I ask again. "What does that word mean?"

"Doppelganger?"

I nod.

Katie shrugs. "Your twin, but like someone you're not related to. They say that there are six people around the world right now who look exactly like you, have the same genetic makeup, but are not blood related to you."

As she talks, an idea starts to form in my head. If there are doppelgangers in one universe alone, and if the universes are all different from each other by only one decision, then there are doppelgangers in all the universes. Maybe even my own.

"Hey, you're hurting me," Katie cries out.

I loosen my hold on her arms, not realizing I was squeezing her. I ask her excitedly, "Do you know anyone who looks like me? Like a doppelganger? Someone who lives in your universe, on earth."

At first, she frowns but then she looks at my face and my body more thoughtfully. "Actually...I think I do," she mumbles.

"Really?" I yell. My voice echoes against the rock bridge, reverberating around us.

Katie nods once. "I mean, if you had shorter hair, you would look exactly like him. He's our age and a cowboy. Walks around in western shirts and a cowboy hat all the time." She rolls her eyes.

But I miss her sarcasm, transfixed at the discovery that I might have found my twin in another universe. What are the chances I slip through the threads to a place so close to my universe doppelganger? "Where is he?" I ask on a choked whisper, hope fluttering wildly in my belly.

"In Ponoka," she replies with a smirk. "Weren't you listening? I go to school with him."

CHAPTER 11

¢

Rattling and clanking wakes me up. My heart beats to fast as I scramble to sit up. Katie groans as she curls up beside me.

It takes me several long breaths before I realize where we are. Exhaustion weighs heavy from last night, and despite my racing mind, I fell asleep. The remnants of the fire from last night are scattered and dry. The rain also has let up sometime in the night.

The most concerning part is the sun. The leaves from the bushes on either side of the bridge glisten and sparkle. The sun is high, the shadow of the bridge almost directly below it.

It must be around noon, I think as I rub my eyes.

"...damn, fool-hearted. Should have stuck to Jenny and High street—Hey!"

This time I'm on my feet. A man—or at least I believe it's a man—is walking toward us from the bush. He is wearing a long robe that is dirty and matted from the outdoors. Plastic flutters around his head from underneath an equally dirty hat.

The noise that woke me came from the cart he is pushing. A metal cage filled with odds and ends. I recognize several bottles and a fur in the pile.

"Hey! This is my spot! Get out of here!" His face is red and eyes wide, the whites showing.

I kick Katies leg gently.

She groans and flips away.

"Katie!" I hiss, making sure to face the oncoming threat.

"It's too early," she moans.

"There's a man here."

That seems to get her attention. Katie rolls onto her feet and is standing beside me in moments. Her curly hair is a frizzy nest around her head. My fingers itch to pull a twig out of the top.

Instead, I turn back to the man.

Katie sighs, rubbing her eyes awake before walking to the motored bike. I shuffle toward her, still not trusting the man.

He stops at the edge of the bridge shadow, glaring at us.

Katie stomps on the pedal and turns a thing.

Click.

And then silence again.

This time I do turn to watch her. Katies frown has deepened as she frantically turns the dial again.

Click.

Click. Click.

Growling, she turns to the body of the bike and unscrews something.

The rattling from the man's cart starts again as he slowly inches toward us. I turn and glare at him. He hesitates.

"Katie!" I hiss, my hands clenching and unclenching.

"I'm trying!" she grumbles. Silence. Then, "Fucking hell," she swears under her breath.

My heartbeat picks up as the hairs on my arms stand on end. I don't like this at all.

I jump a little as her small hand pulls on my elbow. I risk turning away from the man and look down into Katies wide golden blue eyes. "The bike is out of gas," she whispers.

"What does that mean?"

She bites her lip. Then answers slowly, "We have to walk."

Rattling from the cart has me turning back to the man who is now only ten paces away.

I slide my hand into Katies, interlocking our fingers. "Okay." With a squeeze of her hand, I quickly walk to the opposite side of the bridge. The sun hits us like a heat ray.

I turn back once, watching the man greedily run his hands over the bike before finding the click for the seat compartment.

Then Katie is pulling me out of view. She lets go of my hand as she starts scrambling up the steep embankment. I let her go ahead before following, in case of the man.

By the time we reach the top side of the road, both of us are panting and sweating. I can't help but rub my nose. I smell awful.

Turning to Katie, I see her nose scrunched to. Then she flashes me a grin. "Yah, we are pretty ripe right now."

I chuckle.

I don't know if it's from lack of sleep, lack of food, or the stress of running, but the chuckle shifts to giggles. Then we both laugh so hard that we are clutching our bellies. Tears fall to the ground as I finally collapse beside the road.

When we finally quiet, Katie and I share a grin. My chest is warm. Despite everything, her frizzed hair and the streak of dirt on her cheek, I can't help but think she is the most beautiful person I have ever seen. It's in the way her golden blue eyes light up, and that crooked smile of hers.

I want to keep saying things to make her smile and laugh and give me that look she's giving me right now. Like I'm someone good. And worth the trouble that chases me across universes.

"Hey!" a familiar voice calls from below.

Katie reaches her hand out. I take it, letting her pull me up just so I can feel her hand in mine.

"I think that's our cue to hit the road," Katie jokes as she turns and begins walking toward the cityscape ahead of us.

I fall in step beside her, our arms brushing against each other occasionally. Each time they do, a sizzle of heat sparks across my arm and down my back.

The silence between us is comfortable, broken up by the consistent swish of passing cars. I can't help but think that the road is much busier to walk beside than what it felt like when we were driving on it.

"So, we need a game plan," Katie says.

I turn away from the road and focus on the girl beside me. Our fingers brush against each other. I hold my breath. Should I grab her hand?

The moment passes. "I need to pee, so our first step is finding a gas station."

"What's that?" I ask without thinking, forcing my eyes on the road ahead.

Our fingers brush against each other again. It can't have been an accident this time. Did she *want* me to reach out?

Without looking down, I grab her hand and lightly intertwine our fingers.

Besides a slight gasp beside me, Katie does nothing. My heart is racing as a smile bursts from my lips. What is it about this girl that has me acting like I never have around someone I'm attracted to? I'm always the shy one. *Always.* And here I am making the first move—

"You know the place we got the motorbike from? A place like that," she explains.

I nod. "Are you planning on taking another motored bike?"

I watch her as she scrunches her nose. "I don't like stealing..." She looks up at me, "I was thinking of hitching a ride, to be honest. I think we should be safe."

A car honk has me turning to the road to see brake lights and hear squealing brakes from the farthest lane. The larger vehicle with a tank on it seems to be moving slower than what the other cars are used to.

Shaking my head I focus back on Katie. "Besides," she adds, "There probably is a phone at the gas station. So, we can call my mom if we don't find another way back home. She's probably noticed by now that I'm not around..."

I wonder what she means by that. Is her mom absent like my own? What about her dad, or the rest of her family? And it is then that I realize I know nothing about the girl beside me, whose hand I'm clutch like a lifeline.

Before I can say anything, she jerks my arm and points ahead of us with her free hand. "Look! A Husky! It looks like only another kilometer away." She turns and grins up at me, "A good thing because my bladder is really starting to hurt."

I chuckle and shake my head, forgetting the questions that are bubbling up.

Soon we are walking across the bare pavement, a car parked in front of the building and a few larger vehicles near the back at a second building. Katie drops my hand and runs inside. I hesitate in front of the building. I don't need to go to the bathroom. And, as I take a sniff from my arm, I'm slightly embarrassed with how I smell.

I take a seat on the raised pavement in front of the "gas station", as Katie called it, and wait. The sun is still hot as the shadows of the evening slowly crawl across the roadway.

Ding, dong.

I turn slightly to see who is walking out of the building. A grizzled man with a thick grayish beard and a cap on his head walks out. He looks down at me as he's walking. Then he hesitates before stopping.

He looks back at me. "A little late in the day to be wearing pajamas," he says as he takes a sip from the carton cup in his hand. A carton dangles from his other hand.

I shrug. "Didn't have time to get dressed." I don't tell him that it happened days ago and now I simply have no other clothes.

He shoves his cup into the front pocket of his flannel coat, then cracks the carton open. He pulls out a long stick and, from a thing that looks like my pocketknife, he flicks on a flame against the stick. The man takes a long drag from the stick before releasing a cloud of smoke.

In the meantime, I study his appearance while wondering where in the universes Katie is. Despite the heat, the man is wearing a long-sleeved flannel coat, thick jeans, and pointy toed boots. His long hair is pulled back into a low ponytail. I can't tell if he's watching me or not from the dark glasses on his nose.

"Name's Claude. You?"

"Jared."

The man takes another drag. "Well, kid, I'm not sure what you're running from but that's my truck over there." He points behind him to a large vehicle with an even larger trailer behind it. Holes filled the trailer like a cheese grater. For a second, I swear I see something fuzzy poke out of a whole. I blink several times and its gone. "I'm headed down to Ponoka to drop off a load of cattle at the auction mart."

CHAPTER 12

¢

At the mention of the word Ponoka, I jerk up and look at him, my eyes wide. "We're headed back to Ponoka!"

Claude hesitates in the middle of pulling a drag. His brows furrow together.

I quickly stumble through my explanation, "My friend and I—we were having uh, car troubles and we are trying to get back to her home. Which is in Ponoka. Which is where you're going."

Ding, dong.

We both turn and watch as Katie, with her hair slightly tamed and her face clean, walks toward me. She smiles up at me before turning to glance at the man. She automatically steps behind me. I have the strangest urge to pull her into my arms and protect her.

Shaking my head, I turn back to Claude. He watches Katie and I, taking a slow drag before dropping the stick and crushing it under his boot.

"I'm heading out now, so if you want to come with, better come now." He turns and continues walking to the truck.

Before I can follow him, Katie pulls on my arm. I hesitate and look down. Her wide eyes watch Claude as she whispers to me, "Who's that?"

I shrug. "He said he's going to Ponoka with a load of cattle. And he offered to drive us there. You said we needed to find a ride?"

She nods slowly but still watches Claude warily.

I slip my hand into hers, the movement completely natural, and pull her after Claude. The vehicle is much larger than the one Katie had been driving. There are three large steps, well more like ladder steps, to the door. Claude is already sitting in his seat, the low grumble of the engine purring in the afternoon.

We quickly walk around to the other side. I drop Katies hand and climb up to open the door, before clambering in. The inside is huge. Two large seats are in the front, when I glance behind, I see a cot and several lockers behind us. It's bigger than *my* bedroom!

"Would you sit down!" Katie growls from behind me.

Claude chuckles as I plop down onto the seat. Katie clambers in and sees the dilemma, as she hesitates, standing between my legs and seeing only one seat.

"You're small enough you could probably share a seat," Claude mutters as he closes his door and rolls down the window, another smoking stick in his hand.

Katie scrunches her nose before tentatively sitting on my right knee.

Claude shifts the stick around in the middle of the vehicle and the truck lurches forward.

Katie falls back completely in my lap. My arms wrap around her automatically, catching her.

"Seatbelt's over your shoulder," Claude mutters before coughing. He glances out the side window before turning onto the main road, back the way we walked.

Katie reaches behind me and pulls the belt across both of our bodies. I catch a glimpse of her red cheeks before she turns to face forward again. Sitting like this, I'm reminded how small Katie is, her head coming just to my chin, and an extra two inches above of fluffy hair.

Despite our lack of showering, her smell isn't disgusting. There's an intense musk, slightly spicy, that I want to curl into. Another part of my body also likes it. I try to take shallow breaths to control that part, and turn to Claude.

"So, you kids from Ponoka originally," the man asks.

Katie talks for the first time, her voice soft and hesitant. "Born and raised. My mom is waiting for us at the auction."

I stiffen slightly. When did she have time to call her mom? Is she lying?

I feel the sharp sting of her nails in my arm, stopping the questions from bubbling out.

"How about you?" she asks, not looking back at me.

"Oh no, not Ponoka. But from a small town to, just east of Camrose. Kinsella, you heard of it?"

We both shake our heads.

He grunts.

Then we lap into silence. It's not comfortable. But it's not uncomfortable either. I'm searching for something to talk about when Katie speaks up, "You follow the rodeo circuit much?"

Claude chuckles. The sun is streaming through the passenger window as the truck slowly turns off the road onto another one that is heading south. "Bulls and beer? What's not to like. I got Grandstand tickets for the Ponoka Stampede for the past thirty years. They're a good time."

"Yeah," Katie agrees, "a friend of mine, Dwight, competes but he's more into the high school rodeo scene."

Claude turns to us, his eyes wide, as he clucks sadly. "Too bad about that boy. Heard about him. Ponoka born and bred. Hope you gets better soon."

Now it's both Katie and I who turn completely to Claude. What does he mean? Did something happen to my twin—or in Katie's words, my doppelganger?

I interrupt Katie and ask Claude myself, "What do you mean? What happened?"

"You haven't heard?"

We both shake our heads.

Katie adds, "We were friends in elementary school. We kind of grew apart when we hit high school, but I sometimes see him in the halls."

Claude nods to himself, flicking the burning stick out the window and turning the sound dial down to the radio. "Well, a buddy of mine's son competes at the high school rodeos too. Bull rider just like Dwight Erikson. Anyways, during one of the practices, Dwight was dicking around. Not paying attention. Got caught on the wrong side of the bull. Broken ribs, collarbone, an arm, both legs. Boy was damn lucky to be alive."

Katie lets out a shaky breath.

Claude reaches behind him and pulls out a can. He pops the tab and offers it to Katie. She takes it and automatically takes a sip. "Thanks," she mumbles, eyes still on Claude.

She holds the can to my mouth, and I take a grateful sip. We share a glance, the tension hot.

Claude speaks and the tension breaks as we both turn back to him. "Anyhow, boy's been in a coma for over a year. Not sure if he'll ever wake up."

"He at the Centennial Centre?" Katie asks as Claude pulls out a second can for himself.

"Think so. Would make sense since it is the best place in the western provinces for someone with brain injuries to go to."

We lull into a comfortable quiet. Outside the window the city passes by and is replaced by unending hills and fields. Ahead is a long straight road with several lanes filled with vehicles. The sun is hot as it shines in the wide blue sky.

I'm not sure how long it will take to get to Ponoka. And now I'm not sure if the answer is really there. If Dwight Erikson is in a coma, then it won't be possible to talk to him. To see if he really is my twin, my doppelganger from another universe. To know what the hell this all means.

It feels like every time I get close to an answer for the unending race against the Shade, I hit another dead end.

Or maybe I already have hit the answer in one of the other universes I've jumped through and haven't had the time to think about it. It's more than possible. The last three years of life have been constant running. Never any time to settle. To think.

Even now, I'm still worried about the Shade. Did it follow us to the mountains? Is it stuck moving slow in the cold, changing direction? Did it leave this universe?

I don't know.

But I do know that I don't want to stick around long once we get to Ponoka. With Dwight in a coma, there isn't any reason to.

The sun shifts in the sky, glinting across Katies cherry red hair. My fingers tighten around her middle as we bump along the road.

Well maybe there isn't *no* reason. Just no *good* reason.

I can't afford to get sloppy. That's how people die. That's how my dad died.

No. I will make sure Katie gets home safe and sound, and then I will disappear into this world—probably head to the mountains again. After a few weeks, maybe a month, I should be safe again to shift back to Alkira.

Hopefully.

CHAPTER 13

¢

The drive isn't near as long as the stretch through to the mountains. Or to Edmonton on the back of a motorcycle. But it's just as painful.

Each bump in the road shifts the seat, in turn shifting Katies bottom on my lap. The friction is near impossible to ignore, and I'm sure Katie must have noticed by now, despite my best effort.

I keep my gaze focused on the passing bright yellow fields,

trying to think of anything but the warmth of her body pressed up against mine. The tingles of awareness shooting up from my spine. My hands are clenched into tight fists around her waist, keeping her secure, more for my benefit then hers. The first ten minutes of the trip made it obvious that more bouncing and friction is far worse than the constant pressure of her bottom in my lap.

Sighing, Katie leans back, her head leaning against my shoulder. I'm not sure when the cab quieted, so focused am I on my own body's reaction.

"She's a sweet girl," a deep voice mumbles.

Blinking, I turn to Claude. He gives a meaningful look to Katie.

I ignore the heat in my cheeks.

"How long you two been together?"

My ears burn hot as my face flushes. "Uh, we're not together. Not like that."

Claude snorts.

Of their own accord, my fists unclench, and my hands spread across her middle, easily slipping beneath her shirt and finding the warmth of her soft skin. A soft gasp of air puffs against my neck but Katie makes no other move.

Shit.

Swallowing hard, I try to focus on Claude while the rest of my blood runs south. What the hell am I doing?

"We just met. We barely know each other. And—And I don't even go to the same school as her."

The man doesn't say anything, just takes a long drag from his burning stick.

My thumb slowly strokes the skin above her navel. I revel in the softness of her skin, and her curves. It is so unlike the hard muscles of Kian. We have never done more than kiss and cuddle. Yet the warmth of holding Kian is nothing compared to the heat shooting through my veins with Katie sitting in my lap.

"Well don't count yourself out now. Love can grow. My wife and I married only a week after meeting each other. Been happily married forty years this last summer."

I nod along, absently, my mind fixated on the woman in my arms. These feelings feel impossible. Too big. Too immediate. Like a train on track for Vert.

I don't want that. That passion. That big love that I saw in my own parents. I am going to die. Someday sooner than later.

And I have no intention of leaving behind a husk of a human behind when I do die. I can already see it in my head, Katie's bright hair, the same dead look in her eyes like my mom's.

My fingers sink into her skin, gripping her waist.

Another gasp against my neck. And the slightest squirm of her body, lining her bottom up with the hardness of myself.

Gritting my teeth, I turn to Claude.

Before I can say something, anything, to distract myself from whatever is going on between Katies and my body, Claude mumbles, "Looks like we are almost here.

Frowning, I glance out the window as a sign stating Ponoka, two kilometers, passes by.

Thankfully, or not, Katie pops up, no longer feigning sleep as she looks out the window. Her ear tips are red, but she keeps the rest of her face out of my line of sight. "Finally," she breathes out.

"Is it alright if I drop you kids off at A and W? Been craving a burger before I go to drop this load off."

I grunt as she bounces in my lap, nodding to Claude. "That's fine!" Her voice is bright, slightly strained. Or am I imagining that? Is it just me who feels these sparks every time we touch? Every time we are close?

The truck slowly sways as Claude pulls us around and off of the main road and back into the town of Ponoka. In daylight, the drive is completely different than the mad dash through darkness only three days ago.

It feels like so much has happened since that fateful run through the threads. There is so much I have learned from this universe. Cars. Doppelgangers.

Katie.

The heat between us is unlike anything I've dealt with before and I will forever be grateful for the chance at meeting Katie. Now I just need to find a way to extricate myself from her life and keep her safe. And disappear for at least another eleven days.

The lush green fields slowly fall into large buildings. We pass a large sign with a horse welcoming us into town. Not ten meters later, we pass a second sign welcoming us, but with a large black elk on it. On our right is the orange and yellow building with the letters A & W shining on it.

Claude is quiet as the truck belches, jerking back to slow down before turning into the long lane outside of the restaurant.

"Well," Claude starts, reaching down and pulling some bills out of a pocket. He holds out the blue bills to Katie. "This is it. Maybe I'll see you kids at the grounds one of these days."

"Thanks," Katie mumbles as she pockets the papers. She quickly turns and opens the truck door, scrambling down the side of the truck.

For a moment I'm alone with Claude, my lap still tingling from where Katie sat. We share a glance. Claude nods his head meaningfully out the door.

"You hold on to that girl, she's a good one. They don't make them like that anymore."

Ignoring the heat in my cheeks, I mumble, "Will do," and quickly follow Katie out the door.

For a moment we stand in silence, stretching in the hot afternoon sun. Katie is the first to break it. "We should start walking. We can grab something to eat at Tim Hortons."

Frowning, I ask, "Why not here?"

She bites her lip, distracting my thoughts as I focus on their bright red colouring. "I—I just don't want to give that guy the wrong impression," Before I can say anything, she adds, "He's nice! I just want to be safe."

I nod slowly, then without thought, I reach for her hand and pull us away from the truck and farther into town. Katie is quiet as we walk alongside the road.

We end up walking past the Tim Hortons and continuing across the lights that we sped through the first night. A bright yellow **M** calls Katie as she tugs me into the good smelling space. Surprisingly, none of the other people in the building give Katie and I a second glance despite the dirt-stained pajamas and I'm sure our ripe smell.

We get to the front of the line quickly, Katie ordering for me. The smell of grease and bacon has my stomach growling. "I hope you don't mind I ordered for you," she whispers, her other hand playing with our intertwined fingers. The tingles are warm, not as strong as in the truck cab.

I shrug. "I've liked everything you've made or ordered for me so far."

She smiles up at me and for a moment I'm lost in golden blues. Her breath catches. I lean forward. Neither of us looks away, our lips only a breath apart.

"Number forty-four!"

Katie jumps back, letting go of my hand as she turns to the counter. My hand still tingling, I rub the back of my neck and glance around the room. No one seems to have noticed the moment that passed between us.

Taking a breath, I follow Katie as she carries the two bags outside.

"I hope you don't mind walking and eating. I just really want to get home and get in a shower," Katie says as she pulls out a wrapped bundle and hands it to me before opening a second one for herself.

I moan in answer, my mouth aching from the sweet and salty crunch of the hot sandwich.

Katie giggles.

"What is this?" I ask, my mouth full.

"A Big Mac."

I just groan in answer.

We walk up the hill, munching on the first real meal in over a day. Despite the distraction, I can't help but stare at the large building at the top of the hill. The Ponoka Stampede, in red across the top. The building where likely my twin in this universe competed in the high school rodeo, as Katie was saying. And probably the place he had his accident, as Claude said.

By the time we cross the river, waves of déjà vu hit me. Despite the hot sun on our back, I keep flashing back to the black of *that* night. The fear. The uncertainty.

Even now, the hairs on the back of my neck are raised, as if the Shade is still lurking in the small town.

"I'm this way," Katie says aloud, dragging my attention away from the turn that would lead to where Katie picked me up. Instead, we cross to the other side and walk up the cement of a tiny brown house, with a bright red door. Katie opens the door and walks in without a second thought. I hesitate at the door.

"Mom!" she calls out in surprise.

Worried, I shut the door quietly behind me and toe off my shoes. I walk down the short hall and turn to the right. There I am met by the sight of Katie and an older woman embracing.

"... was so worried about you!" the woman says, her voice shaking with relief and fear.

"I'm sorry, mom, things got a little crazy, but I'm alright now."

Her mom holds Katie at arm's length, her face filled with suspicion. Then she glances past Katie, and her eyes widen as she realizes I am standing in the entrance of the small kitchen.

Before her mom can say anything, Katie turns and gestures to me. "Mom, this is my friend Jared. He's in a bit of trouble and needs a place to stay."

Her mom bites her lip, looking just like Katie with her heart shaped face and wide golden blues. Her hair is pulled back into a tight bun, her brown hair streaked with white. She turns back to Katie. "He's not on—"

Katie jerks her head back. "No!" Then she glances at me before answering her mom, "He's clean mom. No drugs, no crime. Just doesn't have a place to stay or anyone to help him out." Then in a whisper she adds, "He's in my grade."

That last sentence softens her mom, her shoulders relaxing as she looks up at me with warm eyes. "Oh dear. I have some extra clothes you can change into. While you two both shower, I can cook up a warm supper before my shift starts."

I nod, mumbling, "Thanks."

Not sure what else to say, I turn to Katie.

But her mom is already grabbing my arm and pulling me back into the hall. Katie disappears from my view, and I'm left alone with her mom.

"So how long have you known my daughter?"

CHAPTER 14

¢

"Mom!" I hear a shout from behind us. My own chest is flushed as my heart beats a wild rhythm in my throat. I've never had to "meet the parents" before. Not that this is meeting the parents in that sense. I'm not dating Katie.

I am with Kian.

Who is in another universe...

Shaking my head, I realize Katie's mom has led me to a plain room with a simple desk and an attached bathroom. She pulls out some clothes from the closet, as well as a bath towel, before setting them on the bed.

Her face is determined as she looks at me.

Before either of us can speak, Katie slides into the room. "Mom!" she shouts again. We both turn to her, Katies face flushed red, matching her flaming red hair. "He's just a friend," she hisses as she pulls her mom out of the room, leaving me alone.

There's more furious whispering in the hall but I can't make out any of it.

I grab the clothes and bath towel and head to the bathroom.

Groaning as the hot water pounds my back, I scrub myself hard with the brush in the shower. Once everything stings, I hit the water to cold and grit my teeth at the temperature change.

This will likely be my last shower. Now that Katie is home, and safe, it is time for me to leave.

Even so, my feet pull me back to the kitchen. Katie is sitting at a table for two, a bowl in front of the empty chair. Her hair is pulled back into twin braids, her face scrubbed clean. She looks young, incredibly young, not the seventeen I know her to be.

"Hey," I say, rubbing the back of my neck nervously.

She glances up from her bowl of granola, then gestures to the empty seat. I know I should say something, to thank her for everything, to tell her I'll be on my way now.

Instead, I pull the chair back and take a seat.

We sit in relative silence, munching on the hard gruel with a white sweet like substance that is unlike anything I've had before. I refill my bowl twice before I finally drop my spoon in satiated hunger.

Katie gets up before I can say anything, clearing the table. Instead of coming back to the kitchen, she walks through a doorway into another space. I follow her and find myself in a tiny albeit comfortable living room. A large couch dominates the space.

Katie is lifting a box toward the black window on the opposite wall. I stare at the space beside her, the only available seating in the room. Maybe I should just sit on the floor?

When the black window lights up, my feet take me into the room and suddenly I'm sitting on the couch, Katie nestled into my side. The screen, like her phone is lit with simple pictures, showing the great blue ocean.

Honk!

I jerk awake, my hands tightening around the warm body snuggled against my front.

Katie groans, shifting back into my chest.

We both realize the moment that a part of me is awake and excited.

I let go of my hold on her waist, the same time she rolls out of my arms, and crashes to the floor. I sit up, glancing down at her splayed body. "You okay?" I growl, my voice scratchy from sleep.

She swallows before wetting her lips, making it even harder to ignore my reaction to her. I grab a pillow from the couch and shove it over my lap.

"I'll be fine," she mumbles, covering her face with her arm.

The screen is still flickering, some nature show about white bears surrounded by endless snow. My eyes move past to the windows, and I'm surprised its beginning to lighten outside. Again.

"How long were we sleeping?" I mutter to myself, rubbing my chest. I need to move before the Shade tracks me back to Katie. Now that she is home safe, it is time to leave before I bring danger to her again.

I turn in time to see Katie pull her phone out. "It's four in the morning." She frowns, her fingers swiping the screen. Finally, she sits up, the early morning lighting the frizzed curls around her braids like a halo of red. She sighs before looking up at me. "Mom's on a double shift. She won't be home till later today. I meant to ask her about Dwight, since Mom works at Centennial Centre. We'll have to wait until she's home to find out what the visiting days and hours are for Dwight."

Right. My doppelganger.

The reason why we are back in Ponoka. Besides keeping Katie safe.

Meeting with Dwight Erikson might give me the answers to why the Shade has been hunting me ever since the first time I walked through the threads.

Katie shifts until she's sitting up, frowning up at me.

"What," I ask as I also sit up on the couch, stretching my arms.

"Today's my dad's birthday," then she pauses for a long moment, staring out the actual window in the living room. "Or it would have been," she whispers, biting her lip.

I rub my chest at the familiar stab of pain. It has been fourteen years since my own dad was taken from me and my mom. I can still see the Shade enveloping him as I fell through the threads to my mom.

I crawl onto the floor and pull Katie into my lap, enveloping her in a warm hug. She snuggles into my chest, sniffling several times. I rock her in silence, giving her comfort as much as she is comforting the pain and loss of my own dad.

Eventually, the morning rays wash across my shoulders, warming us. Her sniffles are replaced by a loud gurgle.

We break apart, her cheeks red with embarrassment.

"I could go for some more of the wet granola we ate yesterday," I say getting up and giving her space.

One more day. By tonight Katies mom will tell us when I can meet with Dwight and then I can be out of their lives. They will be safe again.

I'm not sure how much time we have left before the Shade tracks us back to Ponoka.

Katie leads us back to the kitchen. I grab the same bowl as last night from the rack while

Katie grabs the white stuff and the box of granola. We eat in silence.

She seems far away today. Lost.

I want to take it away, have her smile and be happy again. "Do you do something special on your dad's birthday," I finally ask, taking her bowl and washing it up in the sink.

She jerks in the chair, her eyes clearing as she finally sees me. Katie shakes her head. "My mom doesn't talk about him, ever. She took all the pictures down right after he passed."

I keep my back to her, grabbing a towel and drying the dishes. "Do you *want* to do something for him today?"

Silence.

I put the bowls away and return to the spindly kitchen table, the chair scraping across the floor as I take a seat.

Katie's golden blues are fixed on her hands, her lip caught between her teeth again.

I am right. She looks lost.

"After my dad passed," I start. She jerks up at her eyes widen in surprise at my words. Rubbing the back of my neck, I glance away and continue, "Uh, my mom was a mess after my dad passed. But every year, on the anniversary of when they met, my mom and I would buy a sunflower from the markets and walk down the Seine River. And every time, she would cut the stem. We would hold hands and walk up to my knees into the water and then let the flower go..."

I look back and am caught in her soft gaze.

"That sounds beautiful," she murmurs, rubbing her chest. Her eyes brighten with curiosity. "Is that normal? To mark someone's passing with releasing flowers in a river?"

I shrug.

She doesn't ask again, and we fall into silence again.

"Maybe," Katie starts, and I turn to her, mesmerized by the sight of her biting her lip. "Maybe we could go to the flower store when it opens and leave some flowers for Dad at his grave..."

Frowning, I open my mouth to ask a question. Then I close again. Just as I didn't really want to talk about my dad, Katie didn't really want to talk about hers either.

Besides, I'm not trying to get to know her better. I'll be gone in a day or two, depending on the visiting hours of Dwight.

So instead, Katie disappears into the rooms farther down the hall while I settle in front of the vid screen. Time passes and I'm woken up from my nap by a tickle on my nose. I swipe at it without opening my eyes, my head still foggy with sleep.

A giggle bursts from someone close by.

My heart begins to race as I jump up, and straight into Katies head. We both fall back clutching our heads. I groan as I rub at my forehead. That will leave a bruise.

"Sorry," Katie growls, her eyes still squeezed shut. "I should have just called your name."

She should have. A lifetime of running isn't something I can forget in a quiet moment.

When the pain has subsided enough to just a dull ringing, I finally ask, "What's up?"

She holds out a pair of too large shoes to me. "For the walk."

"We aren't taking a car?"

She shakes her head. "My mom has her car at work and mine is still lost somewhere in the mountains, until the cops or tow truck calls it in. So all we got is two feet. And the graveyard is on the other side of town."

I put the shoes on, watching Katie as she slides a thin folded leather square and the familiar square of her phone into her pocket. "Let's bounce," she calls out as she steps outside. I follow her out as she locks the door behind us.

I'm not sure how long the nap was, but the sun is past the midway of the sky, the heat of the afternoon pressing down on us.

"This way," Katie says, her hand brushing the back of mine.

I shove my hands in my pocket to stop myself from the temptation of holding hers again. For a second a look of hurt crosses her face. Then we are moving.

We walk in strained silence. I'm not sure what to say. I don't want to make it any harder on her when I leave. There is no point in getting closer.

And yet, an hour later we walk out of the flower store with an armful of sunflowers. Katie's smile is bittersweet as she clutches the armful to her chest. I don't try to offer to hold it for her.

By the time we get to the west end of the town, the familiar A and W sign blinking across the road, the silence has settled like a thick blanket over us. On the right, a line of dark pine trees scrape at the sky, rows upon rows of stones winking between the branches.

A heavy darkness settles in my stomach the closer we get. I instantly regret not asking Katie what a grave is.

CHAPTER 15

¢

We turn off the main paved road and walk beside the trees. Katie stays quiet. I keep sneaking glances into the rows of stones. There are indents in some. As if there are pictures or words written on them. The stones themselves are different as well. Some look like a simple, smooth rock. Others are shaped statues. I even see a smooth white stone with what looks to be an animal standing on top.

Rubbing my chest, I try to tamp down the reactions of my body. And my vision.

The threads, which are always there, like glittering dust motes, seem to pulse every time I look into the trees.

A car whiz's by, spitting up rocks toward us. I pull Katie behind me, grunting at the sharp impact on my arm.

"Fucking maniac," she mutters darkly, glaring after the vehicle, before pulling me beside her, her other hand clutching the sunflowers. "Are you okay?" she whispers.

"It's fine," I say. The moment her hand touches my arm, my vision settles and the pounding headache that began without my notice, dissipates.

I watch the furrow in her brow as she turns my arm to get a

better look at the small cut. I slip my fingers into hers and tug her into me.

She gasps, the hard leaves of the sunflowers scratching the back of my hand. Her wide golden blues take me in, soft despite the pain lurking deep within. Her tongue dips out, as her gaze drops to my mouth.

Shit.

I shake my head and take a small step back but still hold her hand. "We should keep going."

She nods, her cheeks red as she pulls us between the large, gated entrance.

The moment we step past the gate, a pulse of energy rips through my body, making all the hairs on my body and the back of my neck stand on end.

I grunt.

Katie looks up at me for a moment, but I keep quiet. Shrugging, she pulls me along the thin sandy road, her gaze focused somewhere deep within the strange park.

The silence is complete between the trees. Not even the lone song of a bird can be heard. It is neither comforting nor restful.

I clutch Katie's hand, walking close beside her, even as I look around myself. As the first stone comes close, I finally can make out the inscription.

Dottie Martha Paddington

1928-1974

Loving Mother, Sister, and Wife

Blinking several times, I look to the next, and the next stone in horror. Names. Dates.

Rows upon rows, the stones stretching out far into the distant tree line.

"What—what is this place?" I gasp out, stopping mid step as another stone comes into view.

The little animal on the stone looks up at me happily as the dates 1953-1954 glare.

Katie frowns at the question, her gaze following mine and landing on the stone animal. "It's a graveyard," she says again. But this time she continues. "It's where we bury our dead."

Bury.

Our.

Dead.

A shudder rips through my back as the reality of what I am surrounded by washes through my mind.

I don't feel the pain as I fall onto my knees. I don't hear the words coming from Katie's moving lips. All I can see is that stone animal looking up at me.

And then I see blue, bright as the sky. Soft and warm as a summer day.

"Jared—Jared!" Katie shouts, shaking my shoulder. Her face is pale, her eyes wide with fear and worry.

I blink several times and look around me again.

But Katie puts her palm on my face and forces me to only look into her eyes. "What's going on, Jared?"

I lick my lips, the pulsing from my mind calms while Katie holds me. "Can't," I finally croak out.

She wrinkles her brow but doesn't ask me anything more. Instead, she gets down onto the hard gravel and wraps her arms around me. It's then that I realize I'm shaking. Sweating.

I bury my head into her shoulder, closing my eyes and focusing on her heartbeat. Long minutes pass.

I finally take my first full breath. The shock is still there, but it's not drowning me right now. I pull back from her slightly, standing up with her still wrapped around me.

Katie squeaks, her legs letting go and falling against mine. I bend down enough so that she can get her feet underneath her. We stare into each other's eyes. No words are said but I can feel her comfort. Her understanding. Her kindness.

And most terrifying of all, I can feel her love.

It's not possible. It *shouldn't* be possible. But it's there. And I feel it rising inside of myself, matching and mirroring hers.

She is a stranger, from another universe. An Otherworlder. I barely even know her. Yet this connection, this trust between us...

Feeling open and flayed, I look away. My eyes land on the discarded sunflowers, some of the petals crumpled from the fall to the road. "We should get those to your dad," I whisper, reaching down for the bundle. My other hand stays firmly intertwined with Katie's. Despite feeling completely vulnerable to her, there is no way that I want to risk being overwhelmed by the strength of the threads in this space.

Never have so many shone so brightly. It feels like large doors instead of just thin strands between universes. The connection is so strong it is overwhelming. And near impossible to look away from.

"Thanks," she mumbles as she takes the bundle from me. We stare at each other for another long moment.

Honk!

We jump, both turning toward the entrance where a car speeds by. The dust washes through the quiet graveyard.

"Let's go," I say, my voice a little shaky but stronger than before. I tug on Katie's hand, until she finally focuses on the road. Then she is the one tugging me along.

There are a few large trees, purposely planted, their long weeping branches fluttering in the wind, both somber and joyful.

Flowers dot the space. We pass a bush of red roses in front of a worn stone, the name barely legible. Across the way is a large garden of petunias and forget-me-nots and peonies.

The flowers are beautiful, a reminder of my mom and all the different flowers my dad would bring to our kitchen table. It always brightened my mom's day. And here, it almost makes me forget the dark truth of the space.

Bury our bodies.

Shuddering, I rub the back of my neck as I stare down at our intertwined fingers. Our own dead are taken by the Council, their bodies burned and released to the wind and sky, in the same way their souls left them. Untethered.

We near the far edge of trees. There aren't as many stones here.

Even the grass has given up and been taken over by a soft layer of moss. Katie pulls us off the gravel and in between a row.

My heart races as my feet sink into the ground. Is there someone beneath me right now? Am I walking on someone's dad, someone's son, someone?

Finally, Katie stops before a large black stone.

Etched in white along its front, it reads:

Thomas Gregory Smith. 1974 to 2004. Loving father and husband. He will be missed.

Katie's fingers loosen their hold, but I can't let go. I clutch them hard, scared to feel the truth of this spot.

Thankfully, Katie doesn't say anything. She takes a step

forward and kneels, placing the flowers in front of the stone.

"Happy birthday, Daddy," she whispers.

Then she stands and curls into my chest. Her body shakes.

I let go of her hand only to wrap my arms around her and pull her in tight. The familiar feel of wetness on my shirt and the sound of broken sobs calms my own racing heart. This I can do. This I know how to do.

I rub slow circles on her back, trying to give my strength to Katie.

As her crying dissipates, a wind begins to pick up. It flutters around us, catching the stray curls around Katies face. It sets the hairs on my arms on end.

"Thank you," she whispers.

I clutch her closer, not wanting her to move away.

Can I really walk away from Katie? I mean, I know I will have too eventually. I can't stay in this universe forever. My *mom* needs me. But whatever this is between us, it feels real. It feels important.

It feels stronger than anything I've felt up to this point, including my time with Kian.

I bite my lip, thinking about Kian.

I can't start anything with Katie, not while I'm still with Kian. To have that unspoken truth laying between us, it would shatter anything I try to build with Katie.

And I want to build. I want to grow. I want to find all the different threads that connect Earth and Alkira. And when the Shade finds me, because it always does, I want to spend my time running from it on earth and not the hundreds of thousands of other universes out there.

Katie breaks through my thoughts as her free hand lays above my heart, gently tapping it.

I grab it with my own palm, intertwining our fingers but holding it to my heart. She sighs, her hot breath skating across my neck. My thoughts start slipping down as my heart begins to race.

"A big part of me hurts, that my dad is gone. But another part of me feels guilty."

Frowning, I rub her lower back with my other hand. My thoughts cool as I wait for her to continue. "Why guilty?" I prompt.

Her thumb skates across my knuckle. The wind picks up and I feel the shiver that wracks through her. I turn us slightly until my back is in the wind and she is cocooned in my embrace.

"Because my real dad is still out there, somewhere," she whispers.

Her words ring in the silence. I wet my lips as I try to find the right words to soothe her. "Blood isn't everything," I finally mumble.

I'm not sure if it helps or not, but she drops a soft wet kiss on my neck. Then another. I pull back just enough so I can look down into her heart shaped face, those golden blues and wild flaming hair.

The blood leaves my mind, making it hard to continue the conversation. She watches my eyes before dropping her gaze to my mouth.

"I know," she agrees, and I can't remember what it is she is agreeing to. My own focus is on that over large top lip. How would it taste? Just one kiss. Then I will keep to myself until I am free to be open to Katie.

"But it's hard to reason with my heart," she adds as she leans in.

CHAPTER 16

¢

My eyes shutter closed automatically as I lean down to her. The barest brush of warmth across my lips has me shivering and tightening my arms around her waist.

Then another whisper.

I growl as she pulls away. My hand comes up automatically and buries into her luscious locks, holding her head steady. Then I lean in and slant my mouth across hers.

Sparks fly across my skin and burn down my back. I can't help but groan. Katy gasps against my mouth and I take the opening. Our tongues tangle as we both shiver with the heat between us. It's like the feeling when I cross the threads, where my body is being pulled apart into a million thin strings and woven back together on the other side. It is both exhilarating and terrifying. But this time I have the heat of Katie's warm body pressed against mine, and I don't feel so alone. In this moment it is both our souls on fire.

Not just my own.

Katie pulls back slightly. I open my eyes but stay close, my forehead against hers. My breathing is as ragged as hers. Her eyes are on mine, searching for I don't know what.

The hairs on the back of my neck are standing, my stomach is a mess. And all I want to do is lean in and lose myself in another kiss.

But her eyes shift. Her brows furrow, her lips pull down in a frown. She pulls back enough to look over my shoulder.

Then her whole body tenses. Her fingers become claws in my shoulders. Her face pales and her eyes widen. Her mouth drops open.

I don't think. I just react.

Lifting Katie into my arms, I squeeze her close as I run between the row of graves toward a strange triangular building in the distance.

"It's—It's—" she stutters, her gaze still caught on whatever is behind me.

But I know what it is. If I my head hadn't been swimming with the taste of Katie, I would have recognized that dread in my gut. The tell-tale cold energy that flowed up my spine and across my skin.

I hesitate long enough at the corner of the building to look over my shoulder to confirm what I feel.

The Shade.

It is the first time I have ever looked at it dead on. Flashes of gray teeth, gray skin, gray leather peek through an endless flaming mist of blackness. Like a great hulking humanoid spider, with long serrated pincers for front legs scrape the earth as it runs to me.

Its movements are jerky, as if it is being pulled apart. The edges of the Shade are blurred.

And then I'm around the corner and setting Katie down.

"Stay here," I whisper as I pull her in for a quick kiss.

She lets me go and stares up at me. I stumble as my mind and body are swept back into the power of this place. *That's why the Shade was slow,* I realize. It was trying to swim through the pull of the threads.

Groaning, I bite my lip until the sting is stronger than the push on my eyes. My vision clears up, as hot blood drips down my chin and the irony tang fills my mouth.

"Jared," Katie whispers, her hand reaching out for me.

But I jerk away from her, and the protection her touch gave me. No way am I pulling her into danger with me. I may not have ever seen the Shade hurt or kill an Otherworlder, but there is always a first time.

And I'm not risking it.

My knees shake as I begin jerkily running back around the corner, this time toward the great weeping tree, and farther into the dead-yard. The trees are taller the farther back I go. The stones more worn. Bushes pop up here and there in front of stones.

Panting, I turn back. The Shade has his serrated claw dug into the dirt to help drag through the pull of the threads.

I stumble and fall onto my back. Before I can scramble to my feet, Katie is throwing something at the Shade. Rocks?

The Shade swings its head and stares at Katie. Her face goes white, but she stares the Shade down.

I know she is fierce, a fighter.

The Shade takes a tentative step toward her.

Freaking out, I look around myself and notice a tipped over vase beside a stone. Swallowing against the bile building up in my throat, I grab the vase and throw it at the Shade.

The vase hits its shoulder, slowly sinking through the matter that makes up the edges of the monster. Not quite solid but not invisible either.

It screeches in agony as it turns back to me.

Swallowing hard, I turn and continue running.

"Watch out!" Katie yells just as something slices my arm.

Grunting, I duck left and into a copse of trees with one large stone at the centre. The strength of the single thread in this spot brings me down to my knees. Tears streaming down my face, blurring my vision, I try to crawl away.

The Shade growls, caught in the same thread as me.

Something slices down my leg, leaving a hot trail of blood. Moments later the pain swells and pulls me down to my chest. I'm panting, trying to just survive. The cold shock of the Shades arm brushing my leg has me puking violently. The last time I was this close to the Shade, my dad pushed me through the threads right as a serrated claw pierced through his back and out his chest.

Suddenly my vision clears, and I'm looking up into golden blues. "Come on!" Katie growls as she pulls my arm and drags me behind her.

I flip over and stumble to my feet. Katie slips an arm under my shoulder, and we hobble as fast as we can. The keening noise coming behind us has all the hairs on my body standing on end.

"Why—Why is it walking so slow?" Katie gasps out as we walk in between gravestones. In the distance I can make out a small stone building surrounded by huge pots of overflowing oranges and red. But the entire building is hazy, even with Kate's shoulder underneath me.

I risk looking back and see the Shade only halfway past the tall stone and trees. "Threads," I mutter.

She stumbles and just barely catches me. "What do you—"

"When a soul leaves the body, the body tethers to the same

place in every other universe. Ever."

Her eyes widen into saucers as she looks up at me, her lips forming a perfect circle. Then, like a light flicking on, she mumbles, "Time stands still when we die." Her gaze slides past me and toward the stone building. She asks in an even quieter voice, "So if multiple bodies are buried in one spot, it means there are multiple tethers of each person to all the universes. Like...like a river instead of a stream?"

I don't answer.

Screeeech.

I break out in shivers, not daring to look back at the Shade that is kicking and screaming its way through the field of threads. "The mausoleum!" Katie yells as she hurries me.

We run, our steps in sync toward the building. The nearer we get, the stronger the pressure of the threads against me. My eyes burn, as I am barely able to keep them open. Just as we get close enough to reach out and touch the building, I realize it has no roof.

We stumble between the bulbous walls covered in silver and chrome squares.

I squeeze my eyes shut and pull Kate into my arms. She wraps hers around my middle and squeezes hard. I can barely make out her words over the rush of thousands upon thousands of threads. Thousands upon thousands of universes. Screams and shouts. Giggles. Honks. Screeches of animals. Explosions—

"Are you okay Jared?"

I bury *my* head in her neck, panting. I can feel Katie turn, her hot breath in *my* ear as she whispers, "The Shade stopped. It's standing just outside the walls of the mausoleum."

Good. If the threads are pulling *my* very being apart into a thousand of a thousand universes, then the Shade stands no chance against it.

A flash of red across *my* eyes has *me* tensing. A breeze on *my* arm. Something wet on *my* left knee.

Katie gasps.

Something warm slides down my neck.

"Your bleeding! I can't see—"

A slice across *my* forehead has me wincing as hot blood drips down *my* temple.

"The universes," I gasp out. I briefly open *my* eyes, catching a glimpse of Katies wide golden blues looking at me with worry and confusion. "My body is being pulled at once into all of them."

"But that means—"

Another slice, this time between my ribs. I grunt, clutching Katie even harder.

"We have to move," she calls, but I can barely hear her over the wind rushing in my ears suddenly.

I follow blindly as she tugs me forward. My fingers ache from how hard I am holding onto her waist. She is the only thing stopping me from being ripped apart into a million universes. From pieces of me being scattered across the worlds.

There is a reason why the places of the dead are sacred.

Why Alkira scatters the remains of the bodies on the wind or in the rivers. To allow so much energy in one spot, even for the normal humans can change people, elementally. Their very atoms feeling the tugs of unseen universes.

It has never crossed my mind that other worlds would *bury* the bodies of their dead. Whole. In one place. All together.

The strength of this place is unlike anything I have ever felt before. And something I wish to never feel again.

With each step, the pressure loosens. The wind quiets. And all I'm left with is the warmth of her body against mine, and her heart beating against my chest.

My shoulders relax as I sigh. I open my eyes, the pressure

finally gone and I smile down into Katies golden blues.

She smiles up at me.

I lean toward her, my gaze sliding down to her lips. My eyes begin to close.

And something both cold and hot slices into my shoulder.

Screeeech!

Gasping, I see Katie for a moment. Then darkness.

CHAPTER 17

¢

Kian's hand is hot in my own, the tingles setting my hairs on end. I can't help the smile on my face as Kian pulls me down a side street. He looks over his shoulder at me, his gray eyes sparkling with mischief.

Before I can think, he pulls me hard to the wall. My arm comes up, caging Kian in between. His hands slide up the back of my shirt. "You should come over to my place after. My dad is out on council business," he whispers as he nips my bottom lip.

I groan, wrapping an arm around his waist and pulling him tight against me. Instead of answering and having to watch the disappointment in his eyes again, I lean down and kiss him hard.

Kian growls against my lips, his hands snaking between us and scratching down my scalp.

"I think I have that T-Gear, it's somewhere back here..." Peter, my mentor's voice, trails off as he disappears to the backrooms of the workshop.

I sigh, stretching my back for the first time in hours. The only light in the room comes from my small work desk hover. Peter focuses on fixing older models of hov-able's as well as hov-crafts in general. We have a lot of older people walk in.

The constant clicks of a fifth cycle clock mark the time. It's what drew me in to Peter's shop. He hadn't had an apprentice in decades. None of the other tinkers from my year were even remotely interested in old-tech. They would rather work on deep space rockets and teleportation portals.

But that clock, to me, is like coming home. It reminds me of my dad.

I rub my chest as my eyes seek out the large circle face at the back of the shop. The hov-able barely illuminates its white face, gleaming off the once shiny ticks.

"...knew it was back here!" Peter's voice breaks through the silence as his bush of gray curly hair pops up behind a stack of broken hovers.

I keep my head down as I leave the school grounds. All the other kids run to the edge of the building where the moms wait to walk them home.

Not me.

Dad hasn't been home in months. And my mom hasn't left her bedroom in just as long.

Oh well.

"Hey, Jared!" a familiar high pitched voice calls.

I sigh, wanting to tell Sae to leave me alone. But I don't. Like me, Sae never has someone waiting to pick her up after school either. I've never asked why. More because I'm scared she will ask me back, and I've never told anyone about Mom. Or Dad.

She bumps my shoulder, her golden blues flashing as she grins up at me. "The results are back. I got in for Knowledge Keeper. What did you get?"

I shrug. "Tinker."

She squeals as she skips around me. I can't help but laugh.

Sae grabs my hands, and we twirl together. Her brown locks are a wild mess, and I think, for a moment, that she's pretty. Like really pretty.

"Hey freak!" a deeper voice calls behind us.

Sae's eyes widen as she drops my hand. Her shoulders are squared and a fire burns in her eyes.

I shove her shoulder back.

She looks up at me in confusion.

I shake my head. Her mouth opens to argue but I'm not there

to listen. I hitch my bag and run the rest of the way home.

I stare at the glowing numbers and short lines that point to each part of the circle. A long stick jerkily steps from tick to tick. Its movement is always the same; never slower, never faster. Despite the three moons shining through into my bed, my eyes are wide as I watch the circle. Or as Dad called it; the watch face.

Dad said it came from a faraway place. And that I must never show it to anyone else. Not even when I finally go to school next year. That it is our secret. And I am his special bug.

My fingers feel along the back, my nail catching on the slight lip. I already opened the back a half dozen times, yet I still open it.

The moonlight barely illuminates the whirring motion of springs and gears that make up the old-tech.

Curious, I carefully crawl out of my bed and toward the warm light of the fire as it seeps through the door frame.

The closer I get to the door, the more I can hear from downstairs. What I thought was the buzz of neighbours going on the night shift, is actually my own parents.

The wristwatch forgotten, I lay my head against the door, straining to make out the conversation.

"...I think I've found them, Alani."

Mom's voice is soft, too soft for me to make out anything.

But my dad is quick to reply. "I have to! I had given up trying years ago. But now, with Jared, I need to find answers. I need to find a way to stop the—"

Crash.

"Pick on someone your own size, you lump of black dirt!"

I blink several times, my eyes taking their time to recognize the blue sky above me. As I turn slightly to the left, I see dark green and black trees swaying in a wind.

And that's when I can suddenly feel the sting of gravel under my palms, the burning heat of blood soaking my shirt on my shoulder. And an ache, soul deep, as if something has pulled out the very pieces that make me who I am. And let go at the last moment before the pieces were completely pulled out.

Screech!

"Come on, you big lump! Over here!"

I blink again, turning to the familiar voice.

And then my blood runs cold. Katie is standing on the other side of the white columned building, her curls a wild flame around her head. Her eyes blazing despite her pale skin and shaking hands as she yells at the Shade.

The same Shade that seems to be caught between me and Katie.

For a moment, I swear the Shade can actually hear Katie. Which I have never seen before. It has never listened to words, or shouts, or anything I have hurled at it before.

It shakes its head as if trying to shake off a leash, but it can't seem to fully turn toward me.

I groan as I roll onto my hands and knees. Everything aches as I stumble to my feet, dangerously swaying to the side. I rub a hand over my eyes, ignoring the hot smear of blood across my face.

"Jared!" Katie screams.

I look up just in time to see the Shade focus its hollow gaze on me again. I watch in slow motion as its claw slowly reaches up to touch me. My soul screams as the memories quiver and loosen their hold inside of me, as if a magnet pulls them closer to the Shade.

"The threads!" Katie screams again. "Grab the threads!"

At first, I don't hear her. All I can see is darkness, and for once fear doesn't shiver through my nerves. Instead, cold acceptance settles through me. To finally be done running. I've been tired, for years, decades if I am being totally honest. And all I want is for it to be over.

I turn to tell Katie goodbye. To look into those golden blues one more time and feel the soul deep connection as the world fades around me.

But a flash flickers in my sight. A thread, tempting and warm.

Without thought, my hand reaches for it.

Just as the Shades serrated claw is millimeters from my shoulder, my own fingers touch the thread.

I gasp as hot and cold rushes through my body. Every piece is torn apart, shaken, and woven back together as I stumble forward. My arms reach out in front of me to try and stop the fall.

I look to the side, trying to catch a glimpse of Katie. Her wide golden blues. Tears streaming down her cheeks. And the Shades serrated claws as it reached for Katie. Through Katie.

Just as my palms connect with cool grass, an unearthly screech tears through the air before being cut off.

Then silence.

Did the Shade get Katie? Is she safe? Or is she bleeding out, life and soul, onto the black dirt of the dead-yard.

My eyes shutter closed, even as I try to turn. To reach Katie. To hold her close to me and protect her.

I *need* to protect her.

But my arms are tired. My body aches. My soul shivers. And all I can do is fall into sleep's cool arms.

CHAPTER 18

¢

Birdsong.

It's the first thing I wake up to.

I try to roll over on to my back, but the movement has me groaning in pain. Instead, I roll to my side. My palms sting, my shoulder aches. And my stomach growls.

That's when I notice the coolness of the grass. Like early morning dew.

But it is afternoon still? When I fell through the thread it was...

Fell through the thread.

I jerk up into a sitting position. My eyes sting from the early morning light as my head swims from the sudden movement. How long have I been out?

As I look around myself, I realize that I am somewhere new, somewhere I have never traveled to before. The grass is longer, swaying in the wind. The trees' circle around the small glade, there depths lost in the darkness.

And most noticeable is the silence of the cars that I got use to in my days on Earth. Maybe I am simply in a park, like when Katie and I camped in "Jasper"?

Blinking several more times, I rub at my eyes and the back of my neck, trying to wake up and get the blood flowing.

The only positive to wherever I have landed, is that the Shade hadn't made it through as well. Katie must have held it back from finding the same thread.

Katie.

Shaking my head again, I push up onto my feet. Wherever I am, I won't need to find food. And hope like crazy that there aren't bears or lions in this forest. With a sigh, I stumble my way to the edge of the glade.

The sun heats my back as it slowly rises higher into the orange and magenta sky. The birds chirp as leaves shudder with their flighty movement from branch to branch.

The moment I enter the trees, everything darkens. The air cools.

I shiver and rub my arms as I continue through the trees. The branches arch and weave together, making it impossible to see the lightening sky. Instead, I'm left navigating through the darkness, following that pull that led me through the last forest to Katie.

Maybe I will find her again.

Likely not...

In all the years that I have fallen and walked through the threads, I have never been able to return to a place I have been before. Except for Alkira. But even then, the threads to Alkira are hidden amongst the other threads, a single star in a galaxy of light.

But there is a first time for everything...

I mean, Earth has been my first time really connecting and affecting another person's life. It is the first time I didn't want to leave behind an alternate universe. It is the first time I noticed someone else *see* the Shade. And the first time the Shade reacted to another person that was not a Wanderer.

I lean against a trunk, just breathing, as the shock slowly wears off.

And with it comes other realizations. Like I will never be able to talk to Dwight, my doppelganger from earth. And I will never see Katie again.

Never kiss her.

Shaking my head, I continue into the darkness, trying to outrun my thoughts. But the pounding of my feet through the underbrush gets me no farther away. Always, she is there. In my mind's eye.

The threads barely shimmer in the forest, damp compared to the beaming streams from the dead-yard.

Suddenly, the deafening silence breaks through my memories. The hairs at the back of my neck rise. My heart begins to beat faster.

I'm not alone in this forest.

Something else, something big, is following me.

I react without thought, rushing straight into the darkness. My shoulder straining, the cut reopening as I pump my arms, clawing at trees. Trying to move faster.

The branches whip my face. My feet stumble over the uneven ground. I catch myself before I fall, cursing under my breath. I can feel *it* close behind me as I push past the underbrush.

I push my legs harder, feeling the burn of my hamstrings singe away the imaginings of golden blues and tear-streaked cheeks. Of a ticking clock face—*where have I seen it before?*

The darkness here is eerie and familiar. My head spins. This feels familiar. I've been here before. In this moment. I've felt this fear. I've been in this darkness. Leaves above me, below me, and all around. My heartbeats that are in time with my pounding feet.

Finally, a lightness. A break in the tree's ahead. The coolness in the air here cloys at my lungs, making it hard to breathe.

At least there is air in this world. Be thankful for the little things.

I shake my head as I realize I've had this thought before.

And then my foot catches on a root. The world tilts as I'm falling. My palms catch me as my body hits the grassy ground.

Heat warms the back of my head.

I flip over onto my back and for a moment I'm taken aback. The sun. It sits high in the sky now.

I sit up and shake my head, feeling like I've been in this glen before. Have I been walking—*running* in circles?

But the silence is still deafening.

Then there's a buzz in the air. A familiar presence.

My arms are shaking even as my heart slows at a familiar scent.

From the darkness, a shadow steps out into the afternoon light. A smile breaks across my face as I recognize that profile. That curly cloud of hair. Those long arms and legs.

My gaze falls on her face, my lips already forming her name.

But then the sun hits her eyes, and I'm stunned as she looks back at me, her blood red eyes nothing like the warm golden blues of Katie.

No, this woman isn't Katie at all...

274. THE HALF SIGHTED

The End, For Now...

The story continues in **The Vampires**

Love reading about strong female main characters? Check out the first book in the completed dark fantasy trilogy...

Ashta the Lion Tamer

Names are power.
The girl knows this.
Now she is Ashta.

Sold into slavery to the kingdom of Tripsia, Ashta chooses to train to be a highly prized guard. A part of the White Lionesses. But she must give up any hope of love. When selected as a personal guard she must learn to balance her sworn duty to protect her charge and want for a life outside of the slave system.

All goes well until she is forced to travel with her charge to the Kingdom of Naankdoen. There she is confronted by her past and must make a decision. Will she give up her life and a chance at love? Or will she protect the ruler of the kingdom that enslaved her?

Start reading at:

books2read.com/u/mezqvZ

Check out the second book in the completed dark fantasy trilogy...

Svetlana the Last Princess

Kings are strong.
Queens are stronger
And heirs outlive them.

Trained to be a highly prized guard, part of the White Lionesses, and the personal guard of Princess Carien, Ashta has failed to protect those most important to her. Watching one of her fellow guards be publicly killed, her heart has hardened. Now Ashta is stripped of her position and used as a bargaining chip between two Kingdoms.

As she tries to stop the war from coming to Tripsia, she begins to uncover the truth of her past. Will she accept who she was born to be? Or will she protect princess Carien at all costs?

Start reading at:

books2read.com/u/49Lzz0

Check out the final book in the completed dark fantasy trilogy...

Darkling the Broken Slave

Born a princess.
Made a warrior.
Always a slave.

Three kings war while their heirs watch from behind gilded cages. A prisoner of war, Ashta has nowhere to go. Forced to watch her father and his armies march to Tripsia, she must learn to harness her powers. But she is too late to save those who had saved her from her father?

Now Ashta must make a choice. Serve—and die—as the slave she had been trained to be? Or fight as the queen she almost was?

Start reading at:

books2read.com/u/b6znnE

Acknowledgements

First off, I would like to thank you, the reader. Without you, this whole process would not have been possible. Writing is a lonely job but knowing that one day it will shape and create worlds for you, the reader, to escape into makes it all worth it. I myself am a reader first and a writer second, and I appreciate the efforts of all the authors whose works of love I have read.

I want to thank the writing community at large. I can't count on my hand how many times I went in search of formatting issues or character development and found a writer who had the answer. We are a small community, but we are mighty! For those of you not published yet, I wish you all the luck on this crazy journey. And know that hard work and dedication pays off. Don't be scared of it.

To Google, thank you for indexing all the answers a crazy author could ever need. I can't count on my hand how many times while I was editing, I would open up a Google search on some crazy random topic or a word I couldn't remember (councillor anyone?).

Thank you to my family, who puts up with my crazy mood swings and doesn't let me get distracted from writing. I know it's not easy dealing with someone with as wide of a creative streak as me. I can't even count how many times you guys took my phone away so I could focus. Jokes aside, knowing you all loved and supported me no matter what I did is a blessing. I appreciate it more than you all can ever know.

To my partner, Austin, who puts up with my procrastination with a laugh and gentle nudge back to my laptop. Thank you for being so kind and supportive. You are the reason I wanted to publish this work in dyslexic friendly font. Every child deserves a book they can read.

About The Author

M. Stamm grew up in central Alberta as the third of four kids. She earned a Bachelor of Communications degree from MacEwan University, in Edmonton, Alberta, in 2017. After graduating, she moved back to her home in rural Alberta so she could focus on her writing while pursuing her Master's in Intercultural and International Communication at Royal Roads University, located in Victoria, B.C.

She grew up reading every book she could get her hands on, for hours on end. This started her love for authors like Tamora Pierce, Rick Riordan, Scott Westerfield, Gail Carson Levine, and many countless more. These sparked her passion for the fantasy genre and sucked her into the endless world of fantasy and science fiction books, which she has yet to emerge from.

Want to read more books by M. Stamm? Keep up to date on new releases on her website *morenastamm.wordpress.com* or Facebook page @StammMorena and Instagram @MorenaStamm.